SOMNIUM

Beyond the Darkness

A.D. STERLING

This is a work of fiction. Any references to people or places are used fictitiously. Names, characters and places are products of the author's imagination, and any resemblance to actual places or persons, living or dead, is entirely coincidental.

ISBN: 978-1-952678-00-4 (pbk)
ISBN: 978-1-952678-01-1(ebook)

www.somniumseries.com

www.adsterling.com

TO MY FAMILY

This story exists thanks to your constant encouragement.
Without you, this would still be nothing but a dream.

CHAPTER 1

Isla frequently wished she were an only child—but not enough to want what happened that day. She was at the kitchen table finishing up her homework after school when her brother Ethan ran into the room wearing a velvet black cloak with a white lining, clutching a pencil.

"Isla! Wanna see something cool?" he asked, bursting with excitement.

She eyed the pencil he was holding, sharpened end up. "You shouldn't be running around with that," she scolded. Isla liked being in charge while their dad was at work, but Ethan often found her enforcement of the "rules" frustrating. In his eyes, she acted more like a strict babysitter than his twelve-year-old sister.

Ethan frowned. "It's a magic trick," he said. "Come on, wanna see?"

Isla sighed and closed her book. Ethan had recently become obsessed with magic. Practically every day he had a new trick to show off. Isla was beginning to find his magician routine tiresome. "Sure. Show me," she said, unenthused.

Ethan's face lit up. "Okay, so you see the pencil I'm holding. Well, what if I just let it go?" With that, he spread open his fingers, but the pencil remained fixed to his palm. "Ta-da!" he said proudly. "It's called the magnetic pencil."

"The magnetic pencil, huh?" Isla said skeptically. "Does that watch you're wearing have anything to do with it?"

Ethan's face flushed red as Isla grabbed his wrist and examined their father's old watch, which looked huge and clunky on a nine-year-old boy. He squirmed as his sister turned his hand over to reveal another pencil jammed under the watchband, holding the "magnetic" pencil in place.

Ethan glared at her, removed his cloak and flopped down into a chair at the kitchen table while Isla resumed her homework. He glanced out the window, blinking in the brightly shining sun.

"Isla," Ethan said after a few moments.

"What?" she asked, sounding annoyed.

"Never mind," he muttered.

Isla felt a pang of guilt as Ethan dejectedly left the table. "No Ethan, it's okay," she replied, her tone completely changing.

"I just thought maybe you'd like to come outside and climb the tree with me," he said hesitantly.

She shrugged and picked up the book she was reading for English class. "Alright."

Ethan's face brightened as he ran outside, grabbed onto the lowest branch and hoisted himself up into the tree. Isla climbed up onto a lower branch, got comfortable, and began reading. Soon after, their father's car pulled into the driveway. He smiled and waved as he headed into the house.

Ethan sang his favorite song as he circled around the tree, hopping from branch to branch.

"That's not how the song goes," Isla said sternly as she glanced up from her book. Ethan shrugged and continued singing, stretching forward to grab the branch in front of him.

Isla tried again. "If you're not going to sing it right, then stop singing."

Ethan again ignored his sister and kept winding around the tree. As he passed by Isla's branch, she reached out and grabbed his arm. She gritted her teeth. "Why can't you just stop?"

Ethan tugged free of her grasp. As his arm slipped from her hand he lost his footing, his legs splitting around the branch beneath him. Tears immediately welled in Ethan's eyes as his skin scraped against the bark. He squeezed his arms and legs around the branch to avoid falling all the way to the ground.

Isla dropped her book and cried out in alarm. "Ethan!"

He narrowed his eyes at her, his cheeks red and wet. "Why did you do that?"

Isla tried to explain away her wrongdoing. "If you didn't pull your arm away you wouldn't have fallen. I didn't mean for you to get hurt."

Ethan refused to accept the half-hearted apology. "You never mean to be mean, but you *are*, Isla. You're mean. M-e-a-n, *mean*." He managed to stand up on the branch and shakily started making his way down the tree.

Isla sat speechless. Their father often told her she was too hard on her brother, but most of the time Ethan just let it roll off his back. Isla had never physically hurt him before, and she began to feel an overwhelming sense of shame.

"Ethan," she called out softly. "I'm really sorry. Are you okay?"

"No Isla, I'm not okay," he said. "Just leave me alone." He stopped when he reached the lowest branch, surveying the best way to get down to the ground.

Isla started making her way down too. "Ethan, wait."

He moved quicker when he saw his sister coming toward him. Ethan grabbed a branch and hung like a monkey for a moment, his legs swinging back and forth as he let go. Upon landing, he winced as tiny pebbles dug into his hands and knees. He clenched his hands tightly and glared at Isla. "You are the meanest sister ever." He ran inside before she could say anything back.

Isla's heart sank. Ethan could be annoying, but he was her brother. She walked into the house, trying to figure out how to make things better. She went upstairs to Ethan's room but found the door locked.

"Ethan, please let me in," she said. There was no response. "I never should have grabbed you. I know it was wrong." Isla held her breath, listening for a response. When none came she exhaled deeply and walked down the hall to her room.

A few minutes later she heard a knock at the door and looked up hopefully, but it was their father.

Isla buried her face into her pillow, worried she'd get in trouble. "I'm really sorry. I didn't mean for him to get hurt." Her voice was barely audible through the fabric.

She felt his hand on her back. "You two really need to work this out. You know you can't do that in here by yourself." He gave her a gentle nudge.

Isla turned her face toward her father. "He won't even talk to me," she said, sniffling.

"Well…would you talk to him if he treated you that way?"

Isla turned her face back to the pillow. "Ethan's right —I am the worst sister ever," came her muffled response.

Isla's father rubbed her back a few times before saying, "You do treat your brother poorly sometimes, but that doesn't make you the worst sister ever. The only way to fix this is to be a better person." He waited for any sort of reaction. When there was none he said, "That my dear, is a choice you must make." He got up and left the room. She could hear him down the hall talking with Ethan and then heard them go into the bathroom.

Ethan was crying. "I don't want to use the peroxide Dad, it hurts."

Isla attempted to sink even deeper into her bed. This was all her fault.

"No Dad, please," she heard through the wall. Isla winced at Ethan's pain. She needed to make this right. She went to his room, grabbed his favorite teddy bear, and took it into the bathroom. As she approached her brother, she tried to make it appear magically from behind his back.

"Ta-da!" Isla said, trying to emulate Ethan's enthusiasm after he performed a magic trick.

He smiled meekly and took the teddy bear. Isla took Ethan's hand. He closed his eyes and squeezed hard. "Okay, Dad."

At dinner that night, things were back to normal as they talked about their day.

"I'm quite sure I know the worst thing that happened to both of you today, so tell me the best thing," their father said.

Ethan perked up. "It was amazing, Dad! At recess today I was playing with my gold coin when my friend Jake asked if he could see it. I held it up like I've been practicing and then made it disappear perfectly before pulling it out from behind his ear. A bunch of other kids asked me to do it to them and I didn't even mess up once."

"Wow Ethan, that's so cool!" Isla said proudly.

"What about you Isla? What was the best part of your day?" their father asked.

"The best part of my day is right now, knowing that you are still willing to talk to me. I hope you can forgive me," Isla said to her brother sincerely.

Ethan shrugged. "You aren't the worst sister ever, Isla. I didn't really mean that."

Their father began clearing the table. "Alright you two, it's time to leave for Isla's dance class." Isla hurried up to her room to change her clothes.

A few minutes later, she came bounding down the stairs, put on her shoes, and found her father in the kitchen doing dishes. "Come on, Dad," she said. "We'll be late." Isla looked in the living room, but it was empty. "Where'd Ethan go?"

Her father dried his hands and yelled, "Ethan, time to go!" Nothing. They checked his room and the basement, but he was nowhere to be found. They went out the front door and checked the tree. He wasn't there either. Isla was getting annoyed.

"Ethan!" she yelled, frustrated. Still nothing. She went around to the back yard and found him swinging, so high that he was almost tipping the legs of the rickety old swing set. "Ethan, now we're late. Thanks a lot." She folded her arms across her chest. "We have to leave for my dance class right this instant. Let's go."

Ethan took one more big swing and let go of the chains as he prepared to jump off. His eyes widened in alarm as he realized he was tipping backwards. He was going to fall! He reached up for the chains, but it was too late. Isla watched helplessly as her brother flailed in the air. She let out a loud scream and ran to the swing set.

Ethan had landed flat on his back with a terrible thud. He laid in the dirt, motionless.

Their father came running around the corner with a panicked look on his face. Ethan's eyes were open, but he wasn't moving. Isla knelt down at her brother's side and grabbed his hand, and their father did the same.

"Ethan?" he asked. The boy still didn't move.

"My head hurts," was the last thing he said before his eyes rolled back.

CHAPTER 2

A week later, Isla was feeling uneasy as she got out of the car in front of the middle school. All of a sudden one of her favorite places in the world was the last place she wanted to be. She was dreading being asked about how Ethan was doing…there wasn't an easy answer to that question.

Isla had spent the previous seven days with her father at the hospital, grief-stricken at the thought that her brother might not recover. When Ethan had fallen from the swing set, he'd landed so hard that his brain had swelled from the trauma to his head. The doctors immediately put him into a medically-induced coma to help protect his brain from any damage. By the weekend, Ethan had been stabilized and the swelling had gone down, but he still hadn't woken. Isla's father felt it was best for her to return to school for some normalcy. But Isla didn't feel normal.

Her best friend, June Li, came around the side of the car and took her hand in support. "Everything's going to be fine," she said. June's grip was strong, but her voice didn't sound as confident.

Isla gave her friend a half-hearted smile. She took a deep breath and started walking, keeping her head down in the hopes that no one would notice her. Isla glanced up as they approached the front door and cringed when she made eye contact with the music teacher, Mr. Wickham. Whenever she saw him she felt a pang of guilt for quitting band in the fall.

"Isla, I'm so glad to see you back at school," Mr. Wickham said, pronouncing the girl's name incorrectly.

"Mr. Wickham, it's *eye*-la."

Isla blushed. June was always correcting their teachers on her behalf because she was too embarrassed to do it herself. Mr. Wickham absentmindedly nodded, his attention already elsewhere as he held open the door for the girls.

"You probably need to stop in here first," June said as they arrived at the counselor's office. "Do you want me to come in with you?"

Isla shook her head no. She gave her friend another poor attempt at a smile and abruptly walked into the office.

Isla's mind was back at the hospital when the sound of the first bell made her jump. The school counselor, Miss Dunn, looked up from her desk before putting down the coffee cup she was holding and quickly walking around her desk to give Isla a hug. "Isla! Welcome back," she said warmly. As she pulled away she examined Isla's face, trying to discern how she was doing. It was all that Isla could take. The scrutiny caused her to break down in tears.

Miss Dunn pulled Isla in tight for another hug, letting her cry. They stood there for a long time until Isla's sobs began to subside. The young counselor shut the door and lead Isla to the couch next to her desk.

"Is there anything I can do for you, sweetheart?" she asked.

Isla really didn't want to start crying again. She shrugged and kept her mouth shut, trying to stave off the tears.

Miss Dunn sensed the storm brewing inside the young girl. She got up from the couch and grabbed a piece of paper off her desk.

"I have your schedule here," she said. "It looks like you should be in health class right now. I spoke with Mrs. Lambert earlier this morning and she told me the class is watching a movie today. If you aren't feeling up to joining in, you're welcome to stay here. You can watch the movie for homework."

Isla gratefully slumped down into the couch. Miss Dunn's computer dinged with a reminder and she glanced at the screen. "I have to step out for a call with your father. I shouldn't be long—we can chat more when I'm done if you'd like."

Isla sunk further into the cushions as the door closed behind the counselor. She heard Miss Dunn say, "Good morning Dr. Rosedale. I have Isla in my office now. Yes, she's doing fine, she just needs some time…" Miss Dunn's voice faded away and Isla closed her eyes, trying to relax. This was the first time she had been alone since the accident, and the peace and quiet felt comforting. It didn't take long for her to fall asleep.

As she dozed, Isla heard humming in the distance. It reminded her of a bedtime song her father would hum to her when she was little. She opened her eyes and was surprised to see a woman with enormous fairy wings smiling down at her. The fairy was practically glowing as the gauzy layers of her dress floated around her. Isla shot up, her eyes darting around Miss Dunn's office, trying to figure out where the woman had come from. The fairy raised her hand and placed a finger to her lips as she continued to hum. Isla immediately felt calmed as the fairy took her hand and led her back to the couch. Something about the fairy felt familiar and Isla peacefully sat with her for a long time.

When Isla heard the doorknob turning, the fairy began fading away. She blinked hard and the fairy was completely gone. The clock above Miss Dunn's desk caught her attention—her second class was about to begin. She stood and began collecting her things. "Thanks for letting me stay here, Miss Dunn, but I really don't want to miss science class."

Miss Dunn kindly opened the door to the office. "Of course. You know you are welcome here anytime if you need to talk."

Isla appreciated the offer but didn't know what she would say to the counselor anyway. All she really wanted to do was get through the day so she could go back to the hospital. She needed to be there so she could apologize to Ethan the instant he woke up.

CHAPTER 3

It had been three weeks since the accident. To everyone's dismay, Ethan was still in a coma. His brain function was normal, so the doctors weren't sure what was causing him to remain asleep. Since he was otherwise perfectly healthy, the doctors at the hospital decided to have Ethan monitored at the Monadnock Sleep Disorder Center. It was founded and run by Ethan and Isla's father, Dr. Michael Rosedale, and his friend Dr. Amit Prasad.

The Center, as they referred to it, was located in a building attached to the hospital by a small corridor. The brick facade of the small structure had ivy climbing up its sides, making it seem out of place next to the concrete sides of the massive hospital next to it. The Center lacked the sterile feel of the hospital, helping give patients a sense of ease as they dealt with their sleep-related problems. Dr. Prasad had taken over care of most of the patients at the Center, including Ethan, so that Michael could focus on his children. Isla knew they were lucky that her father was one of the doctors at the Center, but she quickly discovered that it also meant he got to make his own rules—like insisting that their family stay at the Center until Ethan was able to return home.

It had been a long three weeks, but Isla had gotten used to the daily routine. In the mornings she was picked up by her best friend June's mom. At the end of her school day, she was retrieved by one of the nurses, Rae Geller. The rest of Isla's time was spent at the Center, trying to keep occupied with her homework or playing games while her father nervously hovered at Ethan's bedside.

Despite being bright and cheery, the Center felt less welcoming to Isla since she had been forced to move in. The walls were painted soft shades of yellow and blue and the beds had matching quilts. Above Ethan's bed was a mural depicting farm animals snuggled together, their eyes closed as they slept. At least one teddy bear occupied each chair and the corners were littered with balloons, a few still floating, the rest drooping and deflated. Even though the second bed in his room was empty, it was clear that someone had been sleeping there. A third makeshift bed was a reclining chair laid out with rumpled sheets and blankets. It was a sad reminder that they had all been living in the tiny room at the Center for too long.

Michael approached his son, lovingly pushed aside the brown hair on his forehead and gently kissed his cheek. "Hello Ethan," he whispered before collapsing into the recliner. Ethan didn't move or make a sound.

Isla tossed aside the largest teddy bear she had ever seen and slumped into a chair. She put on her headphones and pulled out a book. Her father's eyes were closed and his breathing was slowing to a low rumble. Isla was exhausted too. Her life had been completely put on hold while she waited for her brother to get better. She hadn't attended any of her dance classes and she barely saw her friends outside of school unless they stopped by, but that hadn't happened much. It seemed everyone wanted to show how much they cared, but then realized how hard it was to see Ethan lying in bed, unresponsive. She couldn't really blame them.

During the first week following the accident, Ethan had been shuffled between rooms in the main wing of the hospital. Each new nurse would ask Isla the same questions, mostly wondering where their mother was. It never got easier telling people that her mom had passed away when she and Ethan were little.

Poor girl, their eyes said, *lost her mother and now she's dealing with another tragedy.* And then the questions would come. "What happened to her?" they asked.

Isla would try to be blunt to end the conversation. "I don't really know. I was only three."

But the questions would always keep coming. "Do you remember her much?" and "Do you have other family in the area?" or "Do you have a stepmother?" Isla's heart broke a little each time she answered no to all of those questions.

She was accustomed to life without her mother, but having people hint at how much their family needed her was the furthest thing from helpful. The only other living relative that Isla knew of was her grandmother on her father's side, and she never visited. Isla received a card on her birthday and a phone call every once in a while, but she hadn't seen her grandmother since her mother's funeral. She had been told that she used to adore her grandmother, but Isla had no recollection of their time together. Besides, she was incensed that her grandmother would just completely disappear from their lives— especially since her dad's own father had left one day and never returned.

Isla's mother was a foster child and hadn't known her birth parents, nor had she ever connected with any of her foster families. The idea of not having a family always made Isla feel sad. She didn't know much else about her mother. It pained her father to talk about her, so Isla rarely asked any questions.

So it was just the three of them now: Ethan, Isla, and their father. It had always been enough for Isla, but lately it felt like she was missing something.

Later that evening, Dr. Prasad stopped by Ethan's room before leaving for the day. Isla watched as he reviewed her brother's chart, knowing there wasn't going to be anything new. He quietly returned the chart to the foot of the bed and frowned to Michael a bit helplessly. With all of the resources at their disposal, it was frustrating that they hadn't been able to help Ethan.

"Until we discover what is causing Ethan to remain in a coma we will continue to monitor his brain waves with the EEG."

Michael didn't look hopeful. They had been running the same tests since Ethan was moved to the Center. So far they hadn't provided any information they didn't already know.

"I'm also going to order another round of bloodwork to rule out any other issues we may have overlooked." Dr. Prasad sighed. "I'm heading home, but I'll be back early tomorrow morning. Good night, Isla," Dr. Prasad said, patting her shoulder as he walked out.

Isla glanced up from her homework. "Good night Dr. Prasad."

A few minutes later, Christopher Hoffman, the other nurse at the Center, came into the room pushing a cart. He was a large man and had intimidated Isla at first, but over time she had come to see him as a big teddy bear. He began by checking the electrodes on Ethan's head and adjusting a few here and there that had come loose. He then followed each wire attached to an electrode and confirmed it was properly plugged into a panel on the wall behind the bed. Isla had once overheard a young patient's mother tell them that they looked like a cyborg and the child's eyes had lit up with excitement. Isla glanced over at Ethan. He didn't look part robot to her, more like a strange science experiment.

When Isla was little, she had believed that the doctors could use these machines to watch patients' dreams, like they were hooking up their brains to a television screen that projected what they were dreaming. As she got older, she learned that what they really captured was nowhere near as exciting. The brain scans reminded her of polygraph tests that she had seen on TV shows, just a piece of paper with a bunch of squiggly lines. She wondered what they learned from those lines.

Isla glimpsed Rae walking towards them down the hallway. Rae was in the middle of her second internship at the Center. During her first internship she'd taken a liking to Ethan and Isla and they became fast friends. She had continued to babysit the kids or take them out for ice cream every now and then, even when she wasn't working for their father. She had volunteered to pick up Isla from school, wanting to help out as much as possible. Rae had even offered to take Isla home with her a few times, just to give her a change of scenery. Isla had been incredibly disappointed when her father had refused, insisting that Isla needed to stay with him at the Center.

Rae poked her head into Ethan's room and Isla grew irritated at the constant commotion. It was difficult to focus when people were always coming and going, and Isla felt a pang of resentment directed at her brother. If he would just wake up they could go home and she could get some privacy again.

"Good evening, Dr. Rosedale. Hey Isla. Would you like me to put in an order with the cafeteria for dinner?" Rae asked.

Isla was sick of the hospital's food and made a pleading face at her father. "Please Dad…can we get out of here and get something decent to eat?"

"I'm sorry love, but you know I can't leave Ethan. How about we order some pizza?" Isla didn't want to argue with him and begrudgingly accepted the compromise.

"Mmmm, pizza. What a great idea," said Rae. "I'll go grab a menu." An hour later, a large pizza had arrived. Isla couldn't believe how good it tasted. After her fourth slice, Isla's belly was full and slightly protruding, but she felt satisfied. Her father put on the news and Isla used the distraction to grab her deck of cards and sneak out to find Rae.

The nurses' station was located at the entrance to the Center and was shaped like a horseshoe with ten patient rooms surrounding it. On each side was a large office, one for each of the doctors.

Lately Isla had taken to sitting at the front desk with Rae to help patients get situated for the evening. She enjoyed greeting their younger patients, handing them coloring books and crayons. The children were often apprehensive, but they quickly warmed up to Isla's encouraging smile.

Isla pulled a chair up next to Rae, who had just returned from a patient. Rae had become like the older sister she always wanted, although they looked nothing alike. Rae's blond, pixie cut hair and blue eyes were a stark contrast to Isla's reddish brown hair and green eyes.

Rae checked her schedule. "Alright kiddo, it looks like everyone is settled in for now. What are we playing tonight?"

"I don't suppose you'd like to join us?" Isla asked Christopher, who was busy at his computer watching patient scans print out next to him.

"Not tonight Isla, but thanks for the offer."

Isla began shuffling the cards like a professional, bending them high into an arch and then sliding them back together. "How about war?" she asked as she dealt the deck into two piles.

"We're in for the long haul tonight then, aren't we?" Rae asked with a wink.

Isla smirked. "Only if we're lucky."

They had been playing for fifteen minutes when there was a low beep from a control panel next to Christopher. He stared at Rae, indicating it was her turn to find the source of the problem. Isla waited patiently while Rae attended to an older woman who had inadvertently disconnected a wire connected to her leg. They continued like that for the next few hours, playing and taking breaks when Rae needed to assist with a patient.

Isla yawned. She glanced up at the clock and noted it was 10:00 p.m. She poked her head into Ethan's room to find her father asleep and snoring. The television was flickering but the sound was down low. Isla turned it off and pulled a blanket over her father. She then got changed for bed and returned to the nurses' station.

Rae stifled a giggle at Isla's expectant expression. "You need your sleep, sweetheart. We'll continue this game tomorrow."

"Ugh. You can hear him snoring from out here. How am I supposed to get any sleep?"

Rae thought for a moment. "Alright, here's the deal. Room 103 is currently vacant, so you can sleep there. It's right across from the nurses' station, so I'll be keeping an eye on you. If you so much as peek out of that room I'll be sending you back to your dad. We both better hope that I'm not pushing his rules too much."

Isla squealed. "You're the best." She jumped up and wrapped her arms around Rae's neck. Then she quietly grabbed her favorite blanket and pillow and hurried to room 103, mouthing "Thank you" to Rae before curling up in the bed. The tranquil silence quickly lulled Isla into a deep sleep.

CHAPTER 4

Ethan was cold. He was at home, but it felt unfamiliar somehow. Things kept changing around him and he couldn't explain why. He was standing at the front door looking down the hallway into the kitchen. The kitchen was yellow when he knew it should be gray.

Weird, he thought. He looked to the right. It should have been his father's office, but on the other side of the threshold was a forest.

Ethan was reminded of the time he had gotten lost in the forest behind the Center when he was six. Michael had brought the children with him to the office on a Saturday morning to finish up some work. It hadn't taken long for them to get bored, so they were sent outside to play in the small park next to the Center. Isla had suggested a game of hide and seek and Ethan jumped at the idea. He offered to hide first, knowing the perfect place.

As Isla counted down from twenty, Ethan ran into the trees. He found a bush and crouched down low. Their father had a strict rule that they not leave the paths in the forest. Knowing this, Ethan figured the best place to hide was as far from the path as possible—Isla would never break the rules to find him. Each time Isla was out of sight, he moved and hid further away.

Eventually Ethan was so turned around he didn't know where the path was anymore. *She'll never find me now*, he'd thought. When he no longer heard Isla's feet crunching the leaves he figured she had given up. Ethan decided to find her and claim victory.

He headed in the direction of what he thought was the Center, but the longer he walked, the more confused he became. After what felt like an eternity he came to a stream he didn't recognize. He was completely lost. He collapsed to the ground in fear and began sobbing. The forest that had once seemed so fun quickly became horrifying. Ethan sat there, scared and alone, shaking uncontrollably as his thoughts drifted to not being found and starving to death before being eaten by wolves. It wasn't until it had started to get dark that the hospital security had finally found him.

The idea of getting lost again was terrifying. He squinted into the forest in his father's office thinking, *If only I could see better maybe it wouldn't be so scary.*

Ethan took a step back when he saw a dark figure watching him from behind a tree, bright yellow eyes glinting, beckoning for him to come forward. As scared as he was, Ethan was just about to step through the doorway when a cool breeze passed through him. He shivered and shook his head as if from a trance.

I should put on something warmer, he thought. He went upstairs to get a sweatshirt. As he entered his bedroom, he felt calmer, but something still seemed different.

Ethan searched for a sweatshirt or a jacket. There was a pile of clothing on the floor, but none of it was his. He picked up a red hoodie he'd never seen before and put it on. He wanted his own clothes, but he was too cold to be concerned with finding them. He looked down to pull up the zipper and was happy to see it was his favorite green fleece. *Magic.*

He thought about how nice it would be to curl up in bed for a little while. He bent down to the pile of clothing in search of a blanket only to discover that the clothing *was* a blanket. He grabbed it and climbed up onto his bed.

Ethan found a tennis ball on the bed next to him. *Odd.* He didn't play tennis. He laid down and started bouncing the ball off the ceiling to see if he could catch it, but he kept missing.

If the ball would just fall slower I'd be able to catch it, he thought. Ethan threw the ball up, only this time it floated down as though it were a feather. He plucked the ball from midair.

That's better, he thought. He tossed the ball up again and watched as it slowly drifted back down, making it effortless to catch. If the ball could float like a feather, Ethan wondered if he could make it fly too. He sat up and threw the ball as far as he could through his bedroom door. He expected to watch it hover above the stairway, but instead it disappeared as soon as it passed through the doorway.

Oh well, he thought.

He listened to the empty house.

Why isn't anyone here? he wondered. Dad was going to be so mad that Isla had left him home alone.

Ethan wrapped the blanket around his body and rested his head on the pillow. He felt tired, but he couldn't sleep. He heard a soft meow coming from the hallway. *Is that a cat?* He saw something that resembled a cat, as if one had somehow been made out of his black velvet magician's cloak. The collar seemed to shape the cat's head, while its belly was white like the satin lining. Its eyes glinted like the gold coins he used in his magic tricks. He watched as the cat paced up and down the hallway. *If only it were real*, he thought.

Ethan tilted his head to the side as he eyed the cat. His mind was playing tricks on him—the cat *was* real.

"Here kitty kitty," he called as the cat cautiously came closer. It meowed again and then jumped on the bed. He lifted up the blanket to let the cat get closer. It began to purr as it snuggled up against Ethan. Its fur was soft and Ethan was happy for the company.

"Your name is…hmm," Ethan said out loud. "Your name is Nox."

The cat appeared to be grinning and Ethan knew he must be right. He picked up the cat. Ethan loved cats, but they never seemed to like him much. His hands often squeezed a little too tightly, but Nox didn't seem to mind. He patted the cat gently and didn't feel so alone anymore. After a few more pats the cat jumped out of Ethan's arms and onto the floor. Ethan was immediately disappointed. He wanted it to stay longer.

"Here kitty kitty," he said again. "Here Nox." The cat stared at him with its bright yellow eyes as it rubbed back and forth against the doorframe.

Ethan slid off his bed and got down on his hands and knees, trying not to scare the cat away. He crawled over and reached out to pat the cat again. Nox brushed against him and purred at Ethan before walking towards the stairs.

It seemed as though the cat was encouraging Ethan to follow it. He tiptoed, thinking if he moved too fast the cat might run off into the forest. Ethan's heart began to race the closer they got to the bottom of the stairs.

"Here, Nox," he said, full of dread. The cat looked over its shoulder at Ethan and ran into the forest. Ethan stopped in the doorway, peering through the trees. The cat had disappeared. Ethan got down low, trying to see from the cat's point of view, but it was no use. He stood up and considered what to do next. He had to help Nox. In the dark forest, it could get lost...or worse.

Ethan knew he needed supplies if he was going to go into the forest. He considered searching the house for everything he'd need, but he wasn't even sure where he'd left his backpack. He turned towards the stairs, and to his surprise, he saw it hanging on the railing.

That's definitely not where I left it, he thought. It didn't matter, it was there now. He opened the bag quickly and was pleased to find it packed with supplies, including a flashlight.

He slung the heavy bag over his shoulders, nearly losing his balance. He stood up straighter to offset the bag's weight. He was just about to go into the forest when he stopped, puzzled by what he was about to do. The feeling of being scared and alone in the forest washed over him and suddenly he couldn't believe he was about to venture into it willingly. Ethan stepped away from the doorway, put down his backpack, and headed for the kitchen.

CHAPTER 5

Isla's eyes flew open as she looked around in alarm. She didn't recognize anything. *How did I get here?*

Something was horribly wrong. *Ethan.* She didn't know why, but somehow she knew that he wasn't safe.

She jumped out of bed and the unfamiliar room swirled around her as though it was coming to life. Her legs buckled and she felt the cold floor beneath her hands. She saw a bright light coming from under the door and she tried to crawl towards it.

Something in the corner of the room caught her attention and she shrieked. There was a monster hunched over watching her with bright yellow eyes!

Isla froze and stared at it, too terrified to move. She tried to work up the courage to run for the door before it attacked.

But what is on the other side of the door? Whatever it was must be safer than being locked inside with a monster, she reasoned. She stared harder, searching for a face around the yellow eyes. The yellow went dark. Was it really even looking at her? Maybe it was asleep. She squinted, trying to adjust to the darkness.

Is that a chair? It was. Isla felt silly for mistaking a harmless piece of furniture for a monster. She stood up, trying again to get ahold of herself.

Panic rose within her again, that feeling that Ethan was in danger. Isla leaned on the bed as her head swirled again and her eyes traveled up the wall. Above the bed was a mural with animals. Isla looked closer. The animals appeared to be moving.

What is going on? She watched as a sheep, two cows, a few pigs, and some chickens moved about their penned in area outside a farmhouse, eating their dinner. Out of the corner of her eye she saw a figure approaching the scene. It was too dark to tell, but she thought maybe it was a fox or a dog. She glanced back at the other animals but none of them seemed to noticed it.

Out of instinct she yelled, "Look out!" All of the animals turned their heads in her direction. Isla leaned away from the mural in disbelief. *This is not possible.*

Movement from within the farmhouse caught her attention. It was difficult to see, but it almost looked like a kitchen. She jumped when she saw a small boy run across the kitchen. Isla blinked her eyes hard and peered at the animals that were still staring at her.

The boy poked his head above the windowsill. "Ethan?" She leaned further toward the mural.

It couldn't be. Now she knew she must be dreaming. He put his finger to his lips, telling her to be quiet.

Isla shook her head. She tried pinching her arm to wake herself up, but it did no good. In the shadows at the edge of the barnyard, the canine was inching forward, eying the animals hungrily. The farm animals had returned their attention to the food, still unaware of the approaching danger.

The canine continued to creep closer as Isla watched, terrified. It stopped moving for a brief moment and then jumped, easily clearing the fence. She dropped her head in her hands, not wanting to see what came next.

Isla's mind raced back to Ethan, worried the canine might go after him next. She peeked through her fingers to look at the bloody scene, but the mural above the bed was no longer moving. The animals were asleep again. It was just a normal painting. Her brother was gone.

Isla pinched her arm again. She was awake. She *knew* she was awake. She felt her eyes blinking, she felt the cold floor beneath her feet. She looked at her bed, at the mural, and at the chair in the corner.

I'm at the Center. She felt calmer as she began to accept that she was safe.

Isla picked up her blanket and pillow to go back and sleep in the other room with her father and Ethan. She quietly opened the door and peered out into the hallway, shocked to see nothing but woods. She took a few steps backward and her pillow and blanket slipped from her hands.

This is simply not possible, she thought. She felt like Dorothy after landing in Oz. Cautiously, she walked into the forest.

CHAPTER 6

Ethan crouched low under the window in the kitchen as he tried to slow his breathing. He felt confused. Beyond the barnyard and through the gate he had seen Isla in the forest. *What is she doing out there?* he wondered. He slowly stood up to look out the window again, thinking maybe he could run past the canine to join his sister. The barnyard was gone. In its place was nothing but trees.

He yelped when he saw yellow eyes glinting at him through the foliage. The eyes seemed to be getting closer and Ethan stepped away from the window. He searched for something he could use to defend himself. He picked up a book from the countertop, thinking he could use it as a shield. He held it in front of his body. It was no longer a book but an actual medieval shield, glinting as the kitchen light reflected off its metal surface. Ethan held his breath as the eyes approached the back door. He exhaled deeply when he heard a meow and saw Nox. His shield banged loudly as he dropped it to open the door for the cat.

"Bad kitty," he said. "Why would you run outside? We don't know what's out there."

Ethan picked up the cat and sat down on the kitchen floor so that Nox could curl up in his lap. He was running through his options as he absentmindedly moved his hand back and forth over the cat's soft black fur. He was terrified to leave the house, but he was lonely and now he was concerned about Isla. The more he patted the cat the less worried he became until his family had slipped from his mind like a distant memory.

"What should we do now?" he asked the cat. Nox purred and rubbed its head up against Ethan's chin.

"I think we've got some old cat toys down in storage. Let's check," he said, the basement door now directly in front of him. *How did I get here?* he thought, somewhat alarmed.

He shrugged and pulled open the door. He was overwhelmed by the strong scent of chlorine. Ethan hurried down the stairs and was amazed to find himself in a large, tiled room with high ceilings instead of their dingy basement. He couldn't believe his eyes. In front of him was an Olympic-sized swimming pool!

Ethan gasped, his excitement growing at having a pool in his basement. Now he could go swimming whenever he wanted! Ethan quickly stripped down to his underwear, not wanting to waste any time with getting a swimsuit. He ran over to the pool and jumped into the deep end.

"Bombs away!"

When he came up for air, he noticed the cat furiously licking off large water droplets from its fur. "Oops... sorry Nox," Ethan chuckled.

Ethan swam to the edge of the pool and held onto the railing. He reached out to help dry the cat off, only to dump more water on it from his hand. Nox ran away in protest.

Ethan still couldn't believe he hadn't known about the pool. He felt like the luckiest kid in town. For a moment he pondered whether or not he'd get in trouble for not having an adult supervising. He could swim, but he wasn't very good at it.

If I can swim from one end of the pool to the other without stopping I can prove I'm good enough, he thought. Ethan cautiously started swimming a front crawl, putting his face in the water as his arm passed his head before turning to take a breath.

About halfway to the other end, Ethan started struggling. He stopped to tread water and catch his breath. He wished he could breathe underwater, then he'd never have to come back up for air. He looked to the edge of the pool and it seemed very far away.

Ethan put his face into the water and started kicking. He kept his head down as his arms pulled past his sides. He rotated his head to take a breath but he accidentally inhaled before his mouth could reach the surface. He felt the water slip down his throat and enter his lungs. He panicked and started coughing. He desperately began kicking. The harder he kicked the less it seemed like he was getting anywhere. He was growing frantic.

Ethan stopped swimming again in order to get his head above water, but it felt heavy, as if he were pushing through mud. He continued to sink further and further below the surface. His lungs were burning. He couldn't stop himself—he took another breath. Ethan wasn't sure what drowning felt like, but he knew this couldn't be it.

Can I really breathe under water? Ethan took a deep inhale of water as though it were fresh air to confirm that he could. He swam deeper, no longer even thinking about drowning.

I could swim all day! He certainly didn't need an adult if he could breathe like a fish. He swam down and touched the bottom like Isla could, where he saw diving torpedoes. He swam around, collecting them all and bringing them to the edge of the pool.

He spun around in circles as he had seen Isla do, enjoying the rush to his head. He wondered how he had gotten tired earlier swimming from one end of the pool to the other, because now it was so easy. He couldn't believe his hands hadn't even gotten pruney yet.

How long have I been in the water? It felt like hours, but he had been having so much fun he didn't want to get out. His eyes darted around to see where Nox had taken refuge from the water. The cat was nowhere in sight. Ethan decided it was time to get out and make sure the cat hadn't wandered outside again.

He climbed out of the pool and sat down on a bench. He looked around for the clothes he'd been wearing earlier, but they were gone. He picked up a towel and began drying off, thinking how nice it would be to have some warm comfy clothes. He felt content when he saw a sweatshirt and a pair of pants appear next to him. He pulled them on quickly and ran upstairs. Nox was waiting patiently in the doorway to the basement. Ethan gave the cat a soft pat on the head, happy to find it safe.

CHAPTER 7

Michael awoke with a start when he no longer felt Ethan and Isla in the darkness. He thought of himself as an otter, holding onto his children while they slept so they didn't float away. In his case, he was keeping their consciousness from floating away to dream. He became anxious when he felt Ethan and Isla slip into Somnium. He had been catching most of their dreams since they were little, but ever since they arrived at the hospital he'd been diligent about stopping all of them. Not once in the past month had he accidentally allowed them to dream.

Michael sat up and squinted through the dark room. Ethan appeared to be sleeping peacefully. He looked over at Isla's bed, alarmed when he realized she wasn't there.

Where is she? Michael rushed to the nurses' station. In his hurry, he accidentally bumped into Rae in the hallway as she was returning from a patient.

"Have you seen Isla?" he asked.

Rae's face turned red. "Yes, sir. I told her she could sleep in room 103. I know it's against your rules and I'm so sorry to have troubled you. She just seemed so exhausted and you were...snoring." Rae gestured at the room next to her, hoping its proximity to the nurses' station would lessen his distress.

Michael sighed with relief. "I need to attend to something in my office. I'll be back shortly."

He rushed down the hallway, shut his office door behind him and quickly picked up the phone to call Dr. Prasad. The phone rang a few times before Amit answered.

"Is everything alright?" he asked briskly.

"I'm not really sure," Michael said. "The children are both in Somnium, dreaming."

"Ah, Ethan's consciousness is finally active again."

"Yes. Well, the thing is...I didn't allow them through to Somnium—at least not intentionally."

"I see. And you fear what their mother saw."

"Do you think it's possible that Shayla really did see the future? If she was right, then they could both be in danger."

"I wish I knew, my friend. For now, I suggest you use your ability to pull them out of their dreams. I will be in as soon as I can."

After hanging up the phone, Michael focused on Isla first. His pupils grew bigger, covering his irises and spreading across the whites of his eyes. He entered the darkness and pulled his daughter's consciousness there with him. He felt her momentarily in the darkness before she woke up and returned to Exsomnis.

Down the hall, Isla threw her hands out in front of her as everything went black. She felt as though the world had disappeared around her and she was floating in space. She squeezed her eyes shut and lurched forward. She screeched when she felt cold metal against her palms. Her eyes flew open and she was staring at the door of a bathroom stall. Her eyes darted around expecting to see the forest, but all she saw was the familiar bathroom at the Center. She walked over to the sink, turned on the water and splashed it on her face.

How did I get here? She leaned on the countertop, staring at herself as she tried to calm down. Isla took one last deep breath in front of the mirror and then straightened herself up.

She pulled open the door to the bathroom and poked her head out. She didn't see anyone so she crept out and started tiptoeing to her brother's room. She backed up against the wall next to room 103, afraid to go in. Holding her breath, she quickly ran into the room to retrieve her blanket and pillow. She stared intently at the floor, refusing to look around lest she see something that wasn't there again. She gave a little shiver, trying to shake the goosebumps off her skin.

With her bedding in her arms, she walked down the hall and quietly pushed open the door to Ethan's room. She was surprised to see that her father wasn't in his recliner.

She knew that she'd definitely get an earful if he found out she hadn't slept in the room last night. But her worry subsided when she figured if he knew she was gone he would have gone looking for her and brought her back.

He must be checking on patients, she thought.

Isla crept over to her brother's bed and was again struck by the feeling that Ethan was in danger. But that was silly. Obviously he was perfectly safe here at the

Center. She gave him a quick kiss on the cheek before returning to her own bed.

She yawned as she glanced at the clock, then frowned...*only one more hour sleep*. She curled up thinking about what had transpired. She didn't often remember her dreams, and this one had certainly been frightening.

Could I have been sleepwalking?

CHAPTER 8

Michael was still sitting at his desk, focused completely on his son. He could feel Ethan's consciousness in Somnium, but he couldn't quite grasp onto it. Michael continued to struggle for a while before he let go of Ethan and the black faded from his eyes. He was baffled. He'd never had such difficulty pulling someone to the darkness. Maybe he was too tired.

Michael got up and headed back to Ethan's room. On his way past the nurses' station he found Rae dozing at the desk. He gave her a gentle nudge to wake her up, giving her a soft, fatherly smile.

"It looks like we could both use a coffee," he said.

Rae sheepishly opened her eyes. "I think you're right," she said, heading towards the coffee machine.

Michael continued down the hallway and quietly pushed open the door to Ethan's room. He was surprised to find Isla in her bed and Christopher standing at the end of Ethan's.

The nurse smiled. "Oh good Dr. Rosedale, I'm glad you're here," Christopher said in a hushed voice. "I saw a jump in his brain activity, so I came down immediately to see if he had woken. Unfortunately, as you can see, he hasn't. But I know you must be pleased to hear that his consciousness is active."

Michael looked at Ethan's bed knowing that this wasn't as wonderful as the nurse thought, but he couldn't tell him that. "Yes, indeed. Why don't you go and pull his brain scan? I'll be out in a moment and we can review it together."

Christopher smiled and nodded as he left the room.

Michael placed a hand on his son, knowing that the physical contact would make his ability stronger. Black covered his eyes and before long he felt Ethan return to the darkness. Michael watched the boy intently, hoping maybe he'd wake up.

Ethan's body remained still. Michael slumped into his recliner, exhausted. He looked at Rae appreciatively when she came in carrying his coffee.

"Thanks Rae," he whispered. "I don't want to fall back asleep."

"Is everything alright?" she asked. She could read the tension all over his face.

"Honestly, I don't know."

Ethan had just gone into his bedroom when everything unexpectedly went dark. At first he had thought that the power went out but when he reached around for the light switch on the wall he couldn't find it. He bent down to crawl along the floor in search of a flashlight, but nothing was there.

Ethan began to panic, flailing his arms and legs. It was as if he was falling and floating at the same time. His breathing quickened.

This feeling of being in darkness, in an empty void, was familiar to him but he didn't know why. He could sense this wasn't the first time he'd been in this strange darkness. He was alone in a sea of nothing, his thoughts the only thing to convince him that he even existed.

And then suddenly his fear begin to subside. His thoughts quieted, as though his brain was shutting down. All he could do was feel. He wasn't scared or alone anymore. He didn't feel pain or worry. In fact, he didn't feel like he had a body at all. He was at peace, as though he were in the safest place in the universe. It was a place he decided he wanted to stay forever. The seconds turned into minutes that eventually became nothing. Ethan's mind slipped into the darkness with not a care in the world.

CHAPTER 9

Isla awoke with a start when she felt a hand on her shoulder gently shaking her. She groggily opened her eyes to see her father standing above her.

"Time for school," he said softly.

"Ugh," she moaned. Then she remembered the previous night and her eyes darted to her brother.

"Everything okay?" her father asked.

Isla thought quickly. She couldn't tell him about last night without admitting that Rae allowed her to break the rules, so she shrugged instead. "Yeah...I just didn't sleep well."

Her father was still looking at her quizzically.

Isla rubbed her eyes. "I better jump in the shower," she said as she grabbed a towel and headed for the small bathroom. She inhaled deeply when the door was closed. It didn't feel right not telling her father.

All this, over a dream, she thought. She told herself she was being neurotic.

Isla showered and got dressed. As she was drying her hair she heard her friend June outside in the hall talking with her father. This was her chance to get out before he questioned her again. Isla raced out of the bathroom, grabbed her backpack, and gave her father a peck on the cheek.

"Have a great day, Dad. I'll see you after school."

He grabbed her arm, stopping her from hurrying away. "You'd tell me if something was wrong?"

Isla plastered a fake smile on her face. "Yeah of course. I just miss my own bed."

He appeared skeptical. "Okay sweetheart. You have a good day."

As the girls rounded the corner, they saw Christopher in the room across the hall, removing wires from a patient. Isla always felt bad for people when she saw them in the morning, electrodes still stuck in their hair, exhausted from a not so great night of sleep. Today she knew how they were feeling.

Before they exited the Center, June held back. "Your dad's right, you do look horrible. Are you sure you're okay?"

Isla's face scrunched up, annoyed at being asked the same question repeatedly. "Yeah, I'm fine," she said abruptly. Then on second thought, she decided to confide in her friend.

"I'm sorry, it's just that I had the weirdest night and I can't tell my dad about it without getting Nurse Rae in trouble. I was sleeping great in a different room until I woke up freaking out that something was wrong with Ethan. I had no idea where I was. And then when I looked in the corner, there was a monster there. Which I know sounds crazy…but honestly, I've never been so scared. All I wanted to do was get away from it and when I figured out it was only the chair I felt so stupid for overreacting."

"That sounds awful," said June, sympathetically.

Isla stared at the ground, a little embarrassed. "I tried to settle down, but then things got even weirder. I swear that the mural on the wall came alive and that Ethan was trapped inside it." As she was recounting the dream to June she realized how silly it sounded.

"I know it all sounds like a bad dream, but I wasn't asleep. What bothered me the most was the feeling that Ethan wasn't safe. No matter how much I wanted to get to him, I couldn't. Of course he's fine, and I know the nurses and doctors are taking such great care of him. It just felt like…something more." Isla felt better talking about it with her friend.

"It sounds like you were sleepwalking. You've never done that before, have you?" June asked.

"I don't think so. I hardly ever remember even having dreams. If I've ever walked in my sleep I didn't know about it."

"Maybe there's a way you can talk with your dad about it without bringing Nurse Rae into it," June suggested. "He *is* the best person to talk to if you're sleepwalking."

"I know. You're right." She should have been honest with her father earlier.

Isla opened the car door and jumped into the back seat. "Good morning Ms. Li," she said to June's mother.

"Good morning to you as well, Isla. Any news today on Ethan?" she asked.

"Unfortunately nothing new." She felt a little dejected knowing this was just the first of many times she'd be saying that today.

Isla rested her head against the window while June and her mother discussed after school plans. She felt a pang of jealousy listening to such a normal conversation. She missed her own activities, especially dance class.

She closed her eyes trying to tune them out. Her pulse quickened when she thought of the mural and Ethan looking back from within the farmhouse. Isla tried to make sense of it all. She opened her eyes when she felt the car come to a stop in front of the school.

It wasn't real, she reminded herself as she got out to start her day.

CHAPTER 10

"Good morning...or should I say good evening?" Dr. Prasad greeted Christopher warmly as he entered the Center.

"It is hard to tell when you work all night," Christopher smirked.

"Anything of interest to report?"

"Ethan's brain scan jumped for a brief period last night, but otherwise no change. Your first patient is in the exam room. I'm headed home for some sleep. Rae is finishing up paperwork if you need anything before she leaves."

Dr. Prasad quickly removed his coat and hurried to the exam room, wishing he had time to talk with Michael first. He grabbed the patient's chart and reread the notes as he opened the door.

"Good morning, Jackson. Mrs. Smith," Dr. Prasad said, nodding in the direction of the boy's mother.

"How are you doing today?" Dr. Prasad asked, noting the boy was Isla's age and wondering if they knew each other.

Jackson looked up from picking at his fingers. "I'm alright I guess."

Dr. Prasad sat down at a small desk in the corner of the room and faced the boy. His kind brown eyes calmed Jackson's nerves a little. Dr Prasad's demeanor always managed to put his patients at ease. "I see you've been having a hard time focusing in school."

Jackson nodded.

"Can you describe for me what it's like for you during the day?"

Jackson surveyed the room as if searching for an answer. "It's like, well…it's like in the middle of class I'll be listening to my teacher when all of a sudden something totally random pops into my mind and the classroom is replaced by whatever I'm thinking about at the moment. Like instead of being in class I'm in the middle of some weird movie."

Dr. Prasad stood up from the desk and moved to sit in a chair next to Jackson. "I want you to try something. Close your eyes with me." Dr. Prasad closed his eyes.

Jackson appeared suspicious, but did as instructed.

"What do you see?" Dr. Prasad asked.

"Nothing," Jackson said, unimpressed.

"Please, keep trying. What do you see?"

Jackson focused on the back of his eyelids. He tried hard to relax. It felt like his mind was expanding outside his head and he heard a cricket. He opened his eyes and searched the room, trying to find the source of the noise. His eyes settled on a cat-sized cricket perched on the desk. He yelped and quickly pulled his arms and legs into his body, attempting to protect himself from the monstrosity.

"Aha, good my boy. It's as your mother suspected… you can see other people's dreams," Dr. Prasad said gleefully. "You are now seeing my dream. It's quite something, isn't it?"

Jackson loosened up, suspiciously glancing from his mother to Dr. Prasad, who still had his eyes shut.

"You're dreaming this?" Jackson reached out to touch the cricket, surprised when his hand passed through it.

Dr. Prasad opened his eyes and Jackson watched as the cricket faded away.

"You and your mother are what we call thetas. You are a daydreamer, to be exact. Thetas have a stronger connection to their dreams than most people. Needless to say, everyone dreams—but thetas can interact with dreams in ways that other people can't. You have the ability to access the dream realm, what we call Somnium, when you are awake. This is why you often get distracted during the daytime, you are being pulled into other people's dreams. Naturally you aren't actually in their dream, but to you it feels as if you are right there with them."

"Whose dreams?" Jackson asked.

"It could be anyone's really, but likely someone who is nearby. Maybe a student who has fallen asleep at school, or somebody else at home sleeping."

Jackson's mouth fell open, unsure what to say.

"I too am a daydreamer," Dr. Prasad continued. "A long time ago I also became distracted by dreams that would disrupt my day. With much hard work, I now am able to focus on specific dreams while awake, but only when I want to. I use this ability to help people better comprehend their sleep disorders."

The boy still seemed bewildered.

"You are fortunate to have a mother who is also a theta, which is why she brought you to me. People with sleep abilities very often pass on their connection to Somnium to their children."

"Why have I never heard of thetas before?" Jackson asked.

"There is a dark history of thetas being persecuted by those who don't understand us. There was a deep fear that if thetas could control the dream realm that one day we would attempt to control the real world too. It wasn't uncommon for thetas, or those suspected to be thetas, to be put to death for being witches. These days most people think we sound like lunatics when we talk about our experiences in Somnium. I would discourage you from discussing this with anyone you don't already know is a theta for that reason."

Jackson's shocked expression was replaced by concern.

"There is no need to worry, my boy. Thankfully we now know what is causing your distractions and making it hard for you to pay attention at school. Over the next few months we will work on controlling your ability. Let this be your first lesson: When you find yourself in someone else's dream again, I want you to close your eyes. Remember that feeling of your world growing—I feel that too. Instead of allowing the world to grow, you must focus even harder to make it smaller. Concentrate on feeling your body and slowing your breathing. Bring your awareness back to yourself so it doesn't get pulled into Somnium."

Jackson wasn't sure what else to say besides, "Okay."

Dr. Prasad felt his watch vibrate indicating his time with Jackson was up. He stood, anxious to find Michael.

"I know you must have lots of questions but I'm afraid we're out of time. In the meantime, your mother can help you learn more about Somnium. We'll schedule an appointment for next week to see how I can help you more. Before you know it, you will have more control over your daydreaming ability."

Dr. Prasad grabbed the boy's chart and headed for the door. "Things will get better for you soon. I promise," he assured Jackson. "It was lovely to see you again Mrs. Smith."

Dr. Prasad hurried down to the nurses' station where he found Michael chatting with Rae. "Ah, good morning my friends," he said. Michael, as usual, looked exhausted. Dr. Prasad glanced at the schedule. "Looks like a normal day."

"Yes," said Rae. "Our patients from last night have all gone home. Since tonight is a night off, all the beds will be empty…" She paused. "Except, of course, for Ethan."

She flipped to the next page and glanced up at Michael. "Dr. Rosedale, your next appointment will be a follow up at 10:00 a.m. with the narcoleptic patient you met with last week."

Dr. Prasad spoke up quickly. "Please, put me on the schedule for that. Dr. Rosedale no doubt will want to stay with his son."

"Yes, of course," Rae said making a note of the change.

"Is that all for now?" Dr. Prasad asked.

"Yes sir." Rae yawned and then stretched. "Is there anything I can do to assist either of you before I leave?"

"Not today. Go home and get some sleep," Dr. Prasad said.

Rae grabbed her purse. "Do let me know if anything changes. I'll stop in when I drop off Isla after school, but otherwise Christopher and I will be back for work tomorrow afternoon," she said as she walked out the door.

Michael turned to his old friend. "I don't like having Ethan here during our routine scans, Amit. I think it may be best if I move him home."

"We've talked about this already and decided staying at the Center is best. If you take Ethan home we'll be unable to monitor him as well as we can here. As the primary doctor on his case I must insist he not be moved."

Michael glanced around to make sure they were alone. "I'm afraid the more patients we have, the harder it is for me to focus and catch only Ethan and Isla in the darkness while still allowing everyone else through to dream. I have never found it difficult to pull someone to the darkness, but I struggled with Ethan this morning." Michael sighed. "I think I'm just too exhausted."

Dr. Prasad was sympathetic. "We know that Ethan should have returned to the waking world by now, to Exsomnis. It's promising to hear that he has left the darkness and went to Somnium, though. That means his consciousness is capable of being active. Perhaps if we allow him to dream we can discover why we have been unable to bring him back to us."

Michael stood up quickly. "Absolutely not," he said firmly. "You know I promised their mother I would keep them out of Somnium. She insisted that was the only way to keep them safe."

"Michael, please hear me out. She told you Ethan would be trapped, yes? If Ethan is trapped anywhere right now, it's in the darkness. I understand more than anyone why you've done what you have. You know I have always supported your decision."

Dr. Prasad wasn't sure Michael wanted to hear what he had to say next. "But...I'm beginning to wonder if keeping him in the darkness is what's best for Ethan right now. Perhaps if we allow him to dream he'll wake on his own."

Michael sat down and put his head in his hands. "I just don't know what is right anymore."

Dr. Prasad was quiet for a few minutes and then said, "Let me spend some time with the boy this morning in Somnium. I will see what his dream realm is like as quickly as I can, and we will devise a plan to help him." Michael didn't move and Dr. Prasad thought for a moment that maybe he had nodded off.

Finally, Michael exhaled deeply. "Okay, but please make it quick."

"Yes, of course." Dr. Prasad retrieved Ethan's chart along with the results of his brain scans. He took a quick pass at the lines and saw the small blip early in the morning where Ethan's brain activity was higher than normal.

This must have been when his consciousness was dreaming in Somnium, he thought. Unlike normal patient scans,

Ethan's were consistently flat because there was so little brain activity happening while he was in the darkness. Seeing a change was encouraging. "I will let you know when I'm done with Ethan. I promise not to take too long. In the meantime, rest my friend."

Michael didn't say a word while he entered the darkness to release his son. Dr. Prasad gently placed his hand on Michael's shoulder and gasped when he saw nothing. He often wondered what it was like for his friend not to dream. He lifted his hand and quietly walked towards Ethan's room.

The black faded from Michael's eyes and he glanced at the clock. It would be torture to count down the minutes that Dr. Prasad was with Ethan. He decided the best he could do was get some fresh air. He exited the Center and sat on a bench facing a small pond.

Michael closed his eyes and let the warmth of the sun wash over his face. He was exhausted and found it tempting to allow himself to sleep, but instead opened his eyes and watched as a duck swam through the pond. Behind the pond was a small wooded park. He considered walking along the paths in the park but worried about getting too far away from the Center.

He was startled to see a small boy come running out of the trees. Michael jumped up from the bench, surprised to see Ethan outside. Just as he was about to run over to his son he saw a man run out after the boy. They were both laughing. Michael knew immediately it wasn't his son. Ethan wouldn't have come out of those woods laughing.

Michael's mind wandered back to the night before. He questioned if his wife had been right in telling him to keep the children out of Somnium. A tear came to his eye thinking about Shayla, and her last few days.

CHAPTER 11

Michael and Shayla were sound asleep in bed, a small three-year-old Isla laying between them. As with most nights, she had snuck into their bedroom and wrapped her arms around her mother's pregnant belly. Isla was excited to feel the movements of her soon-to-be sibling, no matter the time of day. Her mother's breathing quickly lulled her to sleep.

Shayla suddenly sat straight up in bed, Isla's hands slowly sliding off her belly. Michael felt the movement and half opened his eyes.

"Shayla?"

His wife sat motionless. Michael examined her closely. Her eyes were rolled back in her head, her breathing steady and deep. Michael reached out and placed a hand on her arm. He considered waking her up, but he had seen her like this a couple of times recently and each time he pulled her back she was angry.

Isla stirred next to him and opened her eyes.

"Daddy…she so pity," Isla's tiny voice said.

Michael followed his daughter's eyes to the end of the bed but saw nothing.

"What do you see, baby?"

"A faiwy." The little girl grinned. She climbed out of bed and reached up into the air as though she was holding an invisible hand.

"Where are you going, Isla?"

Isla looked up at her invisible friend. "To my bed," she said.

Michael cocked his head to the side, watching his daughter intently. "Isla…you're dreaming."

Isla shot an angry look at her father. "She here Daddy. She's weal."

Michael glanced over at his wife who hadn't moved, the whites of her eyes still visible. He considered walking Isla to her room but didn't want to leave Shayla, and besides, his daughter didn't have far to go.

"Okay sweetheart, you go back to bed then."

Isla glanced up towards the ceiling, her hand still outstretched into the air. Michael followed her with his eyes as she walked down the hallway chatting with the fairy.

Shayla suddenly hunched over clutching her belly as she let out a low groan. Michael, now alarmed, didn't care if he stopped her dream. His eyes became black as he focused on his wife and pulled her to the darkness.

"Shayla, are you alright?" he asked anxiously.

The abrupt transition along with hearing her husband's voice was enough to jar her awake. Shayla's eyes rolled forward, her breathing labored. She reached out and held Michael tightly.

As her breathing returned to normal she let go of him and rubbed her belly. "I'm fine, it was just a small contraction."

"Your eyes were rolled back again," he said, unconvinced.

She shook her head, trying to dismiss him.

"Sweetheart...this has been happening more frequently. It's time you tell me what's going on when you're like that."

"It's a boy, Michael," Shayla said, changing the subject. She placed one of his hands on her to feel the baby kick. Michael leaned down to his wife's belly and kissed where his hand had been.

"How do you know that?" he asked softly.

Shayla took a deep breath. "I didn't want you to worry, but I've been dreaming of the future." She placed her hands on the sides of her belly and then continued. "His future."

"How can you be sure they aren't just your dreams?"

"I'm sure," Shayla said with certainty. "I dreamt I was pregnant when we didn't even know yet. And remember when the doctor couldn't find the baby's heartbeat and we had to go for an ultrasound to make sure it was okay? That's why I wasn't concerned—I already knew he was fine. Everything that I've seen so far about him has happened exactly as I dreamt it would. I have no reason to believe that it's not all true." Shayla's eyes were sad. "I wish I could show you what I've seen."

"Even if I could go to Somnium with you, I don't think I'd want to know the future."

Shayla took his hands again. "Okay, I won't say anything else. But I want you to know that you're a wonderful father. They both adore you so much." She awkwardly leaned forward over her large belly and kissed him on the cheek before laying down and falling back into a deep sleep. Michael laid down facing her, feeling protective of his wife and unborn child. Her dreams worried him.

The next morning Shayla jumped up out of bed and began pacing.

Michael woke with a start and watched as she stopped and gazed out their window into the back yard, letting out a long, "Nooooooo!"

"What happened?"

Shayla wouldn't look at her husband as she said, "I have only ever seen him grow older, but this...this was different." She struggled to string the words together. "I don't know what it means. Why am I seeing these things?"

Michael shrugged helplessly. "If anyone will know why, it'll be my mother. She knows more about thetas than anyone I know, aside from Uncle Marcu. If you're this upset we should go see her immediately."

CHAPTER 12

Michael and Shayla were quiet as they drove to his mother's house. They couldn't help but smile as Isla sang the ABCs from the backseat, frequently singing the wrong letters. Shayla massaged her belly and closed her eyes as she thought about all of the events she had witnessed. She focused on the happy ones, trying to let go of what she had seen that morning.

"We haven't thought much about names," Shayla said, trying to break the tension.

Michael felt uneasy talking about the child, but he wanted to help lighten the mood. "I guess we don't need to worry about girl names."

"Do you have any names you like?" Shayla asked.

Michael thought for a few seconds. "Well...I don't know of any important family names, that's for sure."

Shayla shrugged as she considered the family she never knew. "That makes two of us."

They were quiet again, lost in their thoughts. Shayla stared out the window before she turned and grinned again. "How about Michael Rosedale Junior…we could call him MJ for short."

Michael stuck out his tongue. "Absolutely not."

Shayla giggled. She had known he would never agree to that.

"I've always liked the name Ethan," Shayla said knowingly.

"Isla and Ethan." Michael nodded his approval. "It has a nice ring to it."

"It does, doesn't it?"

As they pulled into the driveway, Michael's mother immediately came rushing outside to open Shayla's door. She gave her daughter-in-law a hefty pull to help her stand up.

"Thank you Miriam," Shayla said, smiling sweetly.

"Oh Shayla, you mustn't be so formal. How many times must I ask you to call me Mim like everyone else?" She then proceeded to the rear door to let out her granddaughter. "My dear little Isla," she said as she gave her a big kiss on the cheek.

Isla reached up to her grandmother. "Mim!" she said excitedly.

Once inside the house, Shayla sank into the sofa in the living room, Michael sitting close beside her, clasping her hand.

"Is everything alright?" Mim asked. "Your call sounded urgent so I cancelled my classes for the morning."

Michael glanced at Isla, who was playing with a set of blocks on the coffee table.

Mim's expression grew anxious. "You aren't here because of…" She glanced in Isla's direction.

"No, no, she's fine," Shayla assured her mother-in-law.

"It's just…" Michael wasn't sure how to continue.

"It's just that maybe she shouldn't hear what we're discussing," Shayla finished.

Michael stood and motioned towards the kitchen so they could move out of Isla's earshot but still be able to see her.

"I don't want you to be alarmed," Shayla began. "The baby's fine…at least he is for now."

Mim's face lit up. "Ah, a boy. I knew it was going to be a boy." She winked at Shayla. "You've been eating so many pickles."

A moment later Mim's expression darkened. "But you said the baby would be fine *for now*. What does that mean?"

"I've been having dreams of his future. Mostly I've just seen him growing older, nothing of real importance."

"Precognitive dreams," Mim said.

"Have you seen this with your students, with other thetas?" Shayla asked.

"I've witnessed it myself at the school, but only once. The student's eyes had rolled back in his head. He foresaw a terrible car accident in front of the school. We all wanted to try and stop it, so for weeks we did everything we could think of to ensure it wouldn't happen. We asked the police to patrol the area more frequently and we put out traffic signs, but nothing we did helped. A few weeks later the accident did indeed come to pass, just as the student had seen. Two people died that day."

"So Shayla really could be seeing the future?" Michael asked. He had expected his mother would tell them Shayla was just dreaming, now he was even more worried.

"It's most certainly possible," said Mim. "I've heard of many other instances of thetas having precognitive dreams."

"Where could they be coming from?" Michael asked, feeling alarmed.

Mim shrugged. "I don't believe anyone really knows. Have any of your dreams actually come to pass?"

Shayla looked down sheepishly. "I've been having the dreams for awhile now. Since just before I found out I was pregnant. Every dream has happened just as I saw it, and I've seen so many yet to come."

Shayla stopped and considered what to say next. "Michael has been adamant that he doesn't want to know the future. I understand if you don't want me to continue."

"I appreciate Michael's apprehension, but I'm not concerned."

Shayla glanced at Michael to see if he wanted to hear the rest. He understood her hesitation and joined Isla in the living room.

"Every dream I've had has centered around him. The first thing I saw was the day I found out I was pregnant. It was the day Isla threw that tantrum at daycare and fell so hard on a wooden toy box that she had to get six stitches above her ear. You thought I was ill from the sight of her blood, but it was really because I was pregnant. That whole day felt like déjà vu to me—I had seen all of it. That's why I took the pregnancy test—after her tantrum unfolded before my eyes I was already convinced I was pregnant."

Shayla rubbed protectively at the baby in her belly again. "All the dreams I've had have been so detailed... they've happened just as I saw them. I have no reason to believe that the others won't too. That's why what I saw this morning scares me so much. I saw an accident, one that is going to put him in the hospital."

"I see. And you wonder what can be done to stop it?"

"I can't help but feel like I'm being shown the future so that I can do something to change it."

"What if by trying to change the future you cause the very thing you're trying to avoid?"

Shayla was quiet as she contemplated the idea. She didn't want to accept that there was nothing she could do to protect her child.

Mim glanced at Isla, who was laughing with her father. "Perhaps you should show me what you have seen and then maybe I can help you decide what should or shouldn't be done. Let's send them out for a walk."

As Michael took Isla around the neighborhood in her stroller, he couldn't help but feel anxious about what was going on in his mother's house.

After a long walk he returned and found Isla had fallen fast asleep. Michael paced in the front yard next to the stroller for quite some time debating if it was best to stay outside and avoid the future, or if he should be inside with his wife. He eventually came to the resolution that she shouldn't be dealing with an uncertain future for their son alone. He decided he would have Shayla tell him everything she had seen.

Michael was about to roll the stroller into the house when he saw that Isla was beginning to stir, making him choose to stay outside instead. He worried that she would wake her mother and grandmother, interrupting their shared dream.

Michael set Isla down on the grass and pulled out a bottle of bubbles from the stroller. The little girl giggled as she ran around trying to pop them all. Michael glanced down at his watch and noted it had been almost an hour since he had left them alone. He hoped that they would be done soon.

In the distance, he heard the faint sound of an ambulance siren. He perked up and listened intently as the sound got closer, watching in horror as the ambulance pulled into the driveway and paramedics hurried into the house.

A few moments later Shayla was rushed outside on a stretcher, Mim close behind. Michael grabbed Isla and gave the girl to her grandmother. "What happened?"

"I think she's gone into labor, but I can't wake her up. She's in so much pain—I'm afraid the baby is coming now."

The EMT stood aside as Michael reached out for his wife. Her eyes were rolling around and her face was contorted in agony.

"You can ride with us, but we have to leave now, sir."

Michael stepped back so they could roll the stretcher into the ambulance, then jumped in. He looked to his mother. "Take Isla home, I'll call you as soon as I can."

Shayla's eyes rolled over and focused on Michael as the sirens blared and the vehicle started to move. She reached out her hand, which Michael quickly grabbed.

"Something's not right." Shayla said as she scrunched up into a ball.

Michael watched helplessly as the EMT prepared a syringe. "I'll give her something for the pain." A few moments later Shayla started to relax.

"I'm not part of the future," she said calmly to her husband. "I see now. I'm not meant to be here." Shayla was looking at him, but also through him at the same time.

Michael stared at his wife in confusion. "You aren't making any sense, what do you mean?"

Shayla's eyes darted aimlessly around the ambulance. She struggled to bring her attention back to Michael and he could tell that her consciousness was still in Somnium. She was sleepwalking. She held his gaze as intently as she could.

"Promise me, Michael. Promise me you won't tell them they are thetas."

"Shayla, I don't understand."

"I…I know you don't want to know the future…" she trailed off.

"It's okay, Shayla. Tell me…tell me what you've seen."

"Ethan…he'll be trapped after the accident, but maybe it'll never happen if you keep him in the darkness…"

Shayla writhed in pain again as the contractions hit her hard. Michael squeezed her hand. She became consumed with her breathing as she focused all of her energy on her contractions. Michael did what he could to comfort her.

It wasn't long before the ambulance came to an abrupt stop and the EMTs opened the doors and jumped out. Michael's stomach dropped as Shayla's eyes rolled back again.

She began rambling. "Ethan isn't like us, he's—different. They will use the children's abilities to bring dreams to life. You can't let that happen, Michael. Ethan and Isla...they will release Iteiri into Exsomnis. It's chaos Michael. The dreams...they're real. Ethan...he's—it's not possible. He wouldn't," she said in alarm. "We have to stop this."

Shayla winced. "Keep them in the darkness, Michael. If they aren't thetas, maybe the Iteiri won't go after them. It's the only way to keep them safe." Shayla was shaking as she watched the future unfolding.

"We have to get her inside now, sir," one of the EMTs said. They pulled the stretcher from the back of the ambulance. Michael watched in horror as Shayla's entire body seized and then went limp.

"We're losing her," was the last thing he heard before she was rushed inside the hospital.

CHAPTER 13

As Dr. Prasad sat down on Ethan's bed, he too was thinking about the day that Shayla died. *Was it possible she had really seen all of this happen?* He pushed the memories aside so he could focus on the present.

He placed his hand gently on the boy. Dr. Prasad's eyes were open but distant and flickering as though a television screen were reflecting off of them. He was watching Ethan's dream as though he were there himself, seeing through the boy's eyes as a silent observer.

Ethan was in a house that Dr. Prasad recognized as the Rosedale family's home, having been there to visit on numerous occasions. He was playing in the kitchen alone. This surprised Dr. Prasad—he wondered why Ethan chose to be alone instead of conjuring a friend. He seemed content so Dr. Prasad didn't feel too concerned. This meant that Ethan wasn't scared to be in Somnium even though he'd been kept from dreaming much of his life.

As Ethan wandered around, Dr. Prasad noticed that the dream house had subtle differences from the real one. He could feel Ethan's interest in exploring, but there was something holding him back. Dr. Prasad couldn't help but wonder why, when Ethan could dream whatever he wanted, he had created something so normal.

Ethan exited the kitchen and rounded the corner, calling "Here, Nox!" Dr. Prasad was dismayed to see a massive forest in place of Michael's tranquil office space. He immediately felt Ethan's apprehension as he stood in the doorway. The forest was dark and foreboding. Dr. Prasad felt the cold breeze against Ethan's cheek and gave a little shiver.

Dr. Prasad felt pleased when he saw a small black cat emerge from the forest and walk into the house. Ethan had created a companion, a pet.

"There you are, Nox," Ethan said as he picked up the cat. Dr. Prasad felt the boy's apprehension melt away when the cat was in his arms.

Ethan walked upstairs to his bedroom where he plopped the cat down on his bed and picked a tennis ball up off the floor. Dr. Prasad watched as the boy moved the ball around in his hands before enclosing it completely. He then moved each hand away from the ball, leaving it to levitate in midair. Dr. Prasad could feel Ethan's satisfaction in performing the trick perfectly.

He continued to watch Ethan play for a few more minutes but decided it was time to tell Michael what he had seen. He removed his hand from the boy and the flickering in the doctor's eyes disappeared.

Dr. Prasad went to the nurses' station to find that Michael had left. He picked up the office phone and dialed his friend to tell him he was done.

Michael appeared at the nurses' station minutes later, a bit flushed from jogging inside. He leaned against the counter, his eyes turning black for a moment as he pulled Ethan back into the darkness.

Dr. Prasad waited patiently until Michael was again focused on him.

"Ethan's dream is actually rather similar to Exsomnis. He seems to have accepted his dream realm as reality. I believe this may be why he hasn't woken yet. He may think he's already awake."

Michael was disappointed. "So how do we wake him up?"

"Perhaps keeping him in the darkness is making it difficult for him to find his way back. He may need more time in Somnium to understand the difference."

Michael sat in silence for a few minutes trying to come up with a different solution. He didn't want to break his promise to his wife. He pushed away from the counter. "I can't leave him in Somnium by himself. We need a better plan before I release him from the darkness again."

"Yes, of course. I understand. We will review all of our options."

CHAPTER 14

Despite Isla's best intentions to be involved in her classes, the hours were dragging. It felt like a full day had passed by before lunchtime. She was dreading the rest of her classes. It certainly didn't help that she was struggling to stay awake. She wanted nothing more than to put her head down on her desk and take a nap.

"I'm so done with today," Isla said to June as they walked to history class.

"I can tell, you look worse than you did this morning."

"Let's hope there isn't a pop quiz," Isla said as the girls took their usual seats next to each other.

Mr. Frazier walked into the room and the class quieted down. "As you all know, we've been studying the American Revolution these past few weeks. Today we are going to watch a film about that era. I urge you to pay close attention and take notes. Spoiler alert—there will be a test on it tomorrow."

This was not good. She was already tired, being in a dark room was the last thing she needed. She loved school and was a good student, but history was her hardest subject. She knew she needed to focus to do well on the test.

Isla pulled out a notebook and a pen as Mr. Frazier hit the light switch and the room went dark. For the first thirty minutes of the movie, Isla took notes furiously in an attempt to stay occupied. Whenever she felt herself nodding off she would shake her head awake. As the movie dragged on, Isla found it harder and harder to keep her eyes open.

She started to think about the scene in the mural on the hospital wall again. She could see it so well it was like she was staring at it again. Isla pinched her arm a few times and wrote down the last few things she heard from the movie, even though they didn't make any sense to her. She tried doodling on the paper, hoping it would at least keep her awake. She drew the farmhouse and a cow, then added in a chicken and the fence. Isla rested her cheek in one hand while her other hand continued to draw. Her pen slowly trailed off and she was out.

Isla was standing outside the farmhouse again. The cows were looking at her with curiosity. The chickens clucked around her feet pecking at the food on the ground and the pigs gave her a few snorts, apparently annoyed by her arrival. Isla surveyed her surroundings, and the forest beyond. There was something ominous about the trees.

She turned to the farmhouse and went inside. As she crossed the threshold, she recognized her own home. Her father was sitting at the kitchen table, engrossed in a book. Isla didn't want to disturb him, so she decided to go up to her room. The hallway seemed incredibly long. No matter how many steps she took she wasn't getting any closer to the stairs.

"Dad?" Her voice was so quiet he didn't hear her.

"Dad, I need to tell you something," she said a little louder. He got up from the table, but he hadn't heard her, and he walked out of her sight.

Isla glanced at the wall at her side. There was a mirror and she saw herself looking back. She touched her face. When she removed her hand, the reflection showed a dent in her forehead. *That doesn't look right*, she thought. She reached up and smoothed it out like putty. *Better.*

Isla felt a hand on her shoulder. It was her father, looking at her expectantly. Isla looked to the mirror, but it was gone.

"What did you need to tell me?" he asked. She began to answer when movement at the end of the hallway caught her attention. She gaped at the familiar glinting yellow eyes.

Isla suddenly felt terrified. She pointed towards the kitchen, but her father was gone. She didn't know what to do. She squinted, trying to determine where the monster had gone, but nothing was there. Isla began tiptoeing down the hall, her heart thumping in her chest.

Isla felt a hand shaking her, but she ignored it. She glanced down at the pen in her hand.

If only it were a knife I could protect myself, she thought. Isla couldn't believe it—it *was* a knife. She didn't know how it got there, and right now she didn't care. She held the blade out in front of her.

Isla felt the hand shaking her again, and this time she heard June hissing "Isla, wake up."

Isla squinted over at June and then up to the television screen in the classroom which was now rolling the credits. She looked down at her hands, worried about the knife she was holding, only to find that she had a death grip on her pen.

Mr. Frazier flipped on the lights and the students started packing up their bags.

"Don't worry," June assured her, "I'll share my notes with you for tomorrow."

"I didn't do anything weird while I was asleep, did I?" Isla asked.

"No, you just seemed like you were having a bad dream. You look like you're about to stab someone with that pen."

Isla glanced down, embarrassed. "You know who I'd really like to stab with this pen?" she said, attempting to make light of the situation.

June rolled her eyes. "As if you'd ever actually do that."

"Yeah, well...Jackson wasn't in class this morning so now I'm going to have to finish our science project alone. I'm not super happy."

A grin spread across June's face. "At least he's cute and smells nice."

Isla stuck out her tongue. "You do realize that's not going to help me get an A, right?"

"No, but it might get you some extra after school time with him."

Rae yawned as she waited in her car for the bell to ring at the middle school so she could bring Isla to the Center. The twenty-year-old nurse was early today, like she was every day. She ran a hand through her short blonde hair, pushing it to the side. She leaned her head on the seat and closed her eyes as she listened to the soft music coming through the speakers. She had gotten used to working every other night at the Center, but that combined with the stress of worrying about Ethan was wearing her out.

Rae focused on her training and slowed her breathing as she transitioned through the darkness and opened her eyes in Somnium. She was standing in a field of wildflowers. This was her favorite dream and she escaped to it whenever she needed a break from the real world. The flowers were so tall that they touched her hips as they swayed back and forth at her sides. The warm sun was shining on her face. Her whole body relaxed and she released all of the tension she was holding onto. She reached down and plucked one of the flowers. Its gorgeous red petals spanned across both of her hands.

She frowned a little when she saw it was slightly wilted around the edges.

Rae willed the flower to heal itself. She felt a tingling sensation in her body as the petals perked up in her hands. She tucked the giant flower behind her ear and bent down to touch the others as she took off running through the open field. The flowers that had previously been drooping flourished under her touch, leaving behind her a trail of perfect blooms. She kept running faster and faster and jumped up high into the air, floating above the field. Rae turned to look at the flowers she had touched and grinned before she quickly spun around and around in the air, sending a whoosh of wind into the field as if she were the center of a tornado.

As her spinning slowed, she was pleased to see that all of the flowers were standing tall and gently swaying from her breeze. She took a deep inhale and smelled the fragrance that had been released. A feeling of happiness washed over her. Rae floated down, stopping when her feet barely touched the ground. She continued tiptoeing through the field, appreciating what she had created.

The car door opened and brought her consciousness back to Exsomnis. Her eyes flew open when she heard Isla giggling. "Caught you sleeping again."

Rae smirked. "How was school, sweetheart?"

Isla was about to slide into the car when she heard someone yelling her name. She was shocked to see Jackson waving with a sheepish grin.

"One second," Isla said to Rae as she pushed the door closed. Her cheeks flushed bright red as she waited for him to run over.

"Hey Isla."

"Hi?"

"So, this might sound weird, but did you fall asleep at school today?"

Isla was mortified—people must be talking about her dozing off in history class.

"I most definitely did *not* fall asleep at school," she lied.

"It's just that I saw you looking in a mirror, and man was it creepy with your face all melty. I figured since your dad worked at the Sleep Disorder Center with Dr. Prasad that...*you know*," he emphasized.

Isla raised an eyebrow, wondering how he knew that detail from her dream. She didn't know what to say. "If you're a patient at the Center this sounds like something you should talk with Dr. Prasad about."

Jackson was dumbfounded. "Oh, okay. Yeah of course, you're right," he said, shaking his head. "I'm sorry I bothered you."

Isla got into the car.

Before she shut the door, Jackson said, "Oh, hey Isla. I'm sorry I missed class this morning. I'm free tomorrow after school to help with the science project if you want."

"Yeah, sure," said Isla. "That'd be great."

The car started inching forward and Jackson quickly disappeared from view.

"What was that all about?" asked Rae with a twinkle in her eye.

"Oh, that's just Jackson. He's my partner in science class and we have a project we're working on together," Isla said dismissively.

Rae turned up the music in the car to allow Isla to decompress from her day without feeling pressured to talk.

Rae could feel Isla tensing as they pulled into the parking lot at the hospital. Isla slowly picked up her backpack and opened the door.

"You know what, I've got a credit at the bakery. How about we stop by for a quick cookie?" Rae suggested.

Isla's face lit up as she emphatically shook her head yes. They walked through the main entrance of the hospital, and then to the bakery where they ordered two warm chocolate chip cookies and chocolate milk.

"Do you mind if we just sit here for a minute?" Isla asked.

"Of course not," said Rae as she sat down at a table next to Isla. She opened the bag and placed each cookie on a napkin.

"It's just that it's so hard going to the Center everyday knowing that Ethan is still..." Isla held back tears as she broke her cookie into bite-sized pieces.

Rae gently rubbed Isla's arm. "I know it's hard."

Isla's eyes welled with tears. "I just feel so responsible. I should have been a better sister."

"Oh honey. I've seen you with Ethan, you're a wonderful sister."

"If only you really knew."

Rae waited for her to continue, but Isla remained silent as she ate each piece of her cookie. "Is there anything else bothering you today? You just don't seem yourself."

Isla's shoulders fell a little as she decided it was best to be honest. "I'm pretty sure that I was sleepwalking last night, and I really don't want to get you in trouble, but I think I should tell my dad."

"Oh honey. Are you worried about my job?"

Isla nodded.

"Isla," Rae said intently, "You need to talk with your father about this."

Isla threw her arms around Rae's neck. "You've just been so good to me. I don't want you to get fired for letting me do something my father wouldn't allow."

"Your dad knows he's hard on you sometimes," said Rae. "He asked me to do what I can to help make things easier on you. Besides, he already knows you were sleeping in room 103 last night."

Isla squeezed tighter. "I don't know how I would have managed living here the last month without you."

"I'll always be here for you. No matter what."

When they returned to the Center, Isla headed straight for her father's office. She told him everything about the previous night and about what had happened that day during class. "It just all felt so real, Dad," she said. "I'm so worried about Ethan."

Isla's father got more and more solemn with each word she spoke about the monster, the mural, and feeling like she needed to help Ethan.

"Dad, say something," she pleaded. "I know it sounds crazy. Please tell me I'm not losing my mind."

Her father hesitated. "You're not crazy Isla. You are a sleepwalker."

"You mean I've done this before?"

Isla's father took a deep breath. "Yes, when you were little. You're like your mother…" He trailed off. "I thought I could control it."

"How could you control my sleepwalking?"

Michael didn't know how to answer her questions without unravelling everything he had worked so hard to conceal. He knew no matter how much he wanted to keep it all hidden that it was too late. "There's so much you don't know, that your mother didn't want you to know." He paused. "I think it's time for you to meet your grandmother. She'll be able to help you more than I can."

Her grandmother? He never wanted to speak of his mother and now they needed her help?

"Dad, what's wrong with me?"

Michael struggled to find the right words. "There's nothing wrong with you, Isla. In fact you come from a line of rather exceptional thetas. Let's call it a skill you didn't know you had."

Isla felt even more lost.

"We all experience sleep differently," he continued. "And some of us, we're called thetas... thetas can control their dreams in ways that others can't."

Isla's eyebrows furrowed. "I don't understand. What does any of this have to do with my grandmother?"

"You know here at the Center we help people overcome their sleep disorders," he said. "Well, your grandmother does something very similar except she teaches thetas how to control their abilities. She has stayed away because she was trying to respect my decision to keep you away from all of this. But now, I wonder if I've made a mistake."

Isla started to laugh. "Wow Dad, I actually believed you there for a minute."

Michael remained somber. "I think it's true that Ethan is in danger, and I'm afraid you may be as well, Isla."

Everything Isla thought she knew suddenly felt like a lie.

CHAPTER 15

Michael shakily picked up his phone and started dialing. Isla watched him closely, listening to the one sided conversation, still believing that this was all some really bad joke. Her father briefly explained what had transpired and simply said, "It's time Isla learned who she is and what she can do. We need your help."

After hanging up the phone, he told Isla, "I know it doesn't make much sense, but I've been keeping you from all of this to keep you safe."

Isla waited for him to break into a smirk and say "gotcha," but his eyes were dark and sad. Isla knew that whatever he was trying to tell her, he believed it was true, and that meant Ethan really could be in danger.

"Dad," she whispered. "Is Ethan like me? Is that why he can't wake up?"

Michael appeared helpless. "I don't know."

The door to the office creaked open and Rae poked her head in. "I'm sorry to interrupt," she said. "I just wanted to let you know I'm heading home." Michael motioned Rae into the office. She looked uncomfortable as the tension in the room swept over her.

"You should know Isla told me about last night," Michael said to Rae. "I've told her that she's a theta."

Isla expected Rae's expression to mirror her own bewilderment, but it didn't. "Wait," Isla said sharply. "Rae knows about this? What's going on?"

Michael went to Isla's side, trying to defuse the situation. "Rae's a theta too. She's what we call a dreamweaver."

Isla was starting to get angry. "So you kept secrets from me...you kept us away from our grandmother, from our only other family. Because of what? Because I'm a sleepwalker?" Isla's body began shaking, she felt so betrayed.

"I'm sorry, honey. Your mother said it was the only way to protect you. I just wanted you and Ethan to feel normal, to live normal lives."

Isla's eyes widened. "So now I'm not normal?" she screamed as she stormed out of the office.

Isla was fuming, and she didn't know what to do with her anger. She ran out the front entrance and just kept running until she was at the edge of the pond outside the

Center. She inhaled deeply and let out a loud yell as she fell to the ground, sobbing.

Soon after, she heard footsteps approaching but refused to acknowledge her father. She curled up into a tighter ball when she felt a hand touch her back.

"I'm sorry this is how you found out," she heard Rae say. "It's a lot to take in all at once, but you need to know that you aren't alone."

As hurt as she was feeling, Isla found she couldn't be mad at her friend. She picked up her head and looked at Rae through her tears. "Why would he keep all of this from me?"

Rae sat down next to Isla and absentmindedly played with her ponytail. "All I know is that he was trying to protect both of you. It's understandable that you're upset, but I'm sure your dad didn't intend to hurt you."

Isla let her head fall on Rae's shoulder. They sat together silently for a while when Rae felt her phone buzz. She read the message and then said, "It's time to meet your grandmother."

"You mean she's here?" Isla asked in disbelief.

"Yep. They're in Ethan's room."

Isla stood, excited and nervous to see her grandmother again after all of these years. She brushed herself off, wiped her eyes, and tried to smooth out her hair.

Rae took her hand. "Ready?"

Isla nodded and together they walked back into to the Center. Isla had butterflies in her stomach as they neared Ethan's room. Rae ushered her in whispering, "You'll be fine," before leaving the family to their reunion.

Michael rushed to his daughter and pulled her in for a hug. "I'm so sorry."

Isla let go of the tension in her body and became putty in her father's arms. "I don't want to be mad at you, Dad." She peeked over his shoulder and saw an older woman with stylishly short white hair and large framed glasses watching intently. Isla gave her a shaky smile and pulled away from her father.

The woman threw her arms around Isla as tears welled in her eyes. "I had hoped we'd be together again under better circumstances," she said to Isla. "But I'm so glad to finally see you again."

Isla awkwardly embraced her grandmother. As they released from their hug the woman kept her at arm's length, examining Isla's face. "You look so much like your mother," she said.

Isla felt uncomfortable under the scrutiny and looked down at her feet. "I don't even remember what I used to call you," she said.

"Well, I'm certainly too young to be a grandmother." She winked at Isla. "My name is Miriam and everyone calls me Mim for short. That's what you used to call me too."

"Okay...Mim," she said as her grandmother pulled her in for another squeeze. Isla had a gazillion questions she wanted to ask. "Mim," she said, hesitating. She turned towards her father. "Dad. Can someone please explain to me what's going on?"

Michael dropped into his recliner.

"Why don't I take Isla for a walk? You stay here with Ethan and get some rest," Mim said to her son.

As they walked out, Isla gave a quick wave to Christopher, who had just gotten out of his car. He waved back as his gaze fixed on Mim. Isla and Mim headed for the benches near the pond and sat together for a few minutes before Mim finally spoke.

"I'm so sorry dear," she began. "This is going to be hard. This story begins on the day your mother died."

Tears welled in Isla's eyes. She had asked her father a few times to tell her the story, but he never could. She stopped asking when she saw how much pain it brought him. She knew this story wasn't going to have a happy ending, but she could tell from the solemn look on Mim's face that it was worse than she had ever imagined.

"I think it's best if I show you, are you okay with that?"

Isla's eyes widened. She expected Mim to pull something tangible, like a photo album, out of her purse. When Mim instead reached out her hands to Isla the girl leaned away with apprehension.

"I want to show you my memories," Mim explained. "I know that probably sounds impossible, but I assure you it's not. If I take us both to the dream realm, what we call Somnium, I can recreate my memories so that you can actually see them."

Isla raised an eyebrow, unsure of what she was agreeing to. "Will it hurt?"

"It won't physically hurt you my dear, but it may be difficult for you to see."

"Okay, I want to go," said Isla, hesitantly.

Mim closed her eyes. Isla felt like she was about to pass out as her field of vision got smaller and smaller. She closed her eyes for a minute until the feeling subsided and then opened her eyes. She was no longer sitting on the bench but was now looking through a doorway at her father. She jumped when she saw a second, younger Mim, next to them at the door of the hospital room.

"Since this is my memory, we aren't actually part of what you see. They won't know we're here. We are just here to observe," Mim said.

Isla looked to her father. He was holding a sleeping baby against his chest as tears rolled down his cheeks. Dr. Prasad was standing at his side with a solemn look on his face. They both glanced up when the younger Mim walked into the hospital room.

"I took Isla home to your babysitter. She was napping peacefully when I left. She's unaware that anything happened to her mother—all she knows at the moment is that she has a baby brother."

Michael gave his mother an appreciative nod before gazing back down at his new son. Ethan.

"Do the doctors have any information about what happened?" Mim asked.

Michael squeezed the baby a little tighter, protectively wrapping himself around the tiny body.

Dr. Prasad stepped forward. "All they could tell us was that Shayla's brain just shut down. They aren't sure what caused it, but they suspect she had a blood clot that led to an aneurism. They tried, but they couldn't save them both."

Mim approached her son. "I'm so sorry," she said.

Michael choked up as he handed the baby to his mother. He stood up, walked to the window and stared out of it for a long time. He helplessly placed his hands in his pockets as he turned around.

"There's something you should know," he said to Dr. Prasad. "Shayla began having precognitive dreams shortly after she got pregnant. I just found out about it. This morning she saw something that terrified her, so we went to visit Mim."

Dr. Prasad gave Mim a concerned glance.

"What happened inside the house?" Michael asked his mother.

Tears fell from Mim's eyes. "Shayla wanted to show me what she had been seeing, so we went into Somnium together. Many of the visions were just of the children as they grew older. But as she said, her last vision was different. Ethan was in a hospital, unconscious. That's all I saw before I was unexpectedly forced from her dream. Her water had broken and she was writhing around in pain so I called 911. I tried to wake her up, but I couldn't pull her back."

Mim cleared her throat. "She wanted to believe there was a purpose to what she was seeing, that there was something she could do to change the future. I disagreed."

"She told me that I had to protect them both by keeping them from dreaming. She said the children can't know they are thetas. In the ambulance she was having another vision," Michael said. "She was speaking nonsense. She said the children would bring dreams to life."

Dr. Prasad seemed uncertain. "That can't be possible."

"If she saw it, I'm afraid it very well may become a reality," said Mim.

Michael began to sob. "She said she wasn't part of the future. Could she have known she was going to die today?"

Mim was shocked. "Oh, how awful."

They were all silent for quite some time.

"What will you do?" Mim asked her son solemnly, fearing the answer.

"I have to keep the children in the darkness as much as I can."

Mim shook her head. "What Shayla saw will happen no matter what you do. If the children are prepared…"

Michael interrupted. "She said it's the only way."

"I'm sorry Miriam, but I agree with Michael," said Dr. Prasad. "We must heed her warning."

"But this is who they are, it's who we all are. I can't hide who I am from them. I won't." Tears were running down Mim's cheeks. "Thetas are my life…the school is my life. The only way I can help you hide this from them is if I keep my distance."

Mim choked up. "This accident will happen Michael, and when it does I fear for the children. If you change your mind I will be there. Until then…" Mim kissed the baby on the forehead, handed him back to her son, and rushed out the door.

CHAPTER 16

Isla was back on the park bench looking at Mim, tears gently rolling down her cheeks. She felt a weight settle upon her from knowing what happened that day. "So that's why you stayed away from us?"

"And that's why you've had so few dreams. We all did what we thought was right to protect you, but now it would seem your father can no longer keep you from Somnium. It's time you learn more. May I take you there again?"

Isla nodded. Mim closed her eyes and Isla felt that same sensation of being about to pass out. She accepted it this time and when she opened her eyes she was standing next to Mim in a whimsical make-believe room.

The high ceiling was draped in billowing pieces of white fabric that dropped elegantly down to the floor at the corners. The walls were adorned with a mishmash of frames and mirrors and there were varying sized doors all around that made Isla wonder if they would take her to magical places like in *Alice in Wonderland*. The only light in the room came from tiny orbs floating around them like fireflies. Isla caught an orb in her hand, surprised to find it was cool to the touch. She gently tossed it back up into the air and watched as it floated away.

Mim was now wearing a very stylish looking black pantsuit and her white hair was a spiky bright blue. Isla looked down and noticed her body was completely normal, down to the clothes she had already been wearing.

"Would you like to be wearing something different, dear?"

Isla said the first thing that popped into her mind. "I really miss dancing." Mim nodded sympathetically and suddenly Isla was wearing a black leotard and white tights like she would wear to a dance class along with a smart looking purple shrug around her shoulders and matching leg warmers. Isla smiled and did a few plies.

"So, this is Somnium?" Isla asked. "Where exactly are we?"

"When we are awake our consciousness is in Exsomnis, but when we sleep our consciousness moves to Somnium. That is, with the exception of thetas like your father. Dreamcatchers can only go to the darkness, so for that reason they never dream. Everyone else has their own dreams when they sleep, but I have the ability to go wherever I want in Somnium. I can go into anyone's dream whenever I choose, and I can take any theta with me as long as I know them. For this reason they call me a sandman. We are now in my dream."

Isla gestured to the doors. "What's behind them?"

"These are entrances to my dreams. Doorways often serve as a transition from one dream to another. Shall we go through one?"

Isla approached a tall door that looked like it belonged in a castle and examined it curiously.

"Excellent choice, my dear." Mim turned the doorknob and the two stepped through. As they crossed the threshold Mim morphed into a small child wearing a princess dress and tiara. They were standing in a flower garden outside a huge castle.

Isla crouched down and examined the little girl. "Mim?"

Her grandmother giggled and bobbed her head up a down. "This is where my brother Marcu and I used to come, and it's still one of my favorite dreams." She spun around in her dress to make it flare out and then stopped to pluck a handful of grass. Mim tossed it up into the air.

As the blades swirled around their bodies Isla felt it tickling her all over.

The girls collapsed in a pile of laughter as they clutched at their sides. Isla grinned at her grandmother, finding it funny to see her behave so childlike.

Mim took off running and stopped when she was standing in the middle of a patch of moss. She reached up to take Isla's hand. "Now jump and make sure you reach up as high as you can."

Isla crouched down and leaped into the air. When they landed back on the ground, they were sent flying into the sky as though they had just jumped on a trampoline. They kept going up higher and higher, high enough to touch the clouds. Isla raised her free hand above her head and felt the fluffy cloud—grabbing a handful. Panic set in as they started to descend.

Isla felt Mim's tiny hand squeeze hers. "It's okay."

Isla risked a glance down and found that they were surrounded by a bed of clouds, slowly floating downwards.

"Try a bite."

Isla brought the cloud she was clutching to her mouth and licked it. She raised her eyebrows at her grandmother. It tasted like cotton candy.

"It's good, right?"

Isla nodded enthusiastically. "This place is amazing—so why doesn't anyone talk about it? Why didn't I know that thetas exist?"

"Thetas have been around practically forever," little Mim said. "People became afraid of us, and sometimes when people are afraid they do mean things. So now we keep our abilities secret to protect ourselves."

Isla felt a little lightheaded as they reached the ground and the cloud slowly disappeared like a fog. "This is unreal. I feel like I'm awake. How will I ever know if I'm dreaming or not?"

"No matter what dream you're in, you will always have control over yourself," Mim explained. She raised her small arms in front of her body and crossed them. Isla watched in amazement as they passed through each other. She raised her own arms and imagined them doing the same. A satisfied smile crossed her face when she was able to make one arm pass through the other as if it was a hologram.

"Obviously you'll only ever be able to do *that* in Somnium," Mim giggled.

"Have you always known you were a theta?" Isla asked.

"When I was little," she gave a little curtsey, "I could make my brother fall asleep with me and I would bring us here. It was a way for us to escape a sad childhood." The castle and the flower gardens were gone, replaced by a dusty and dank bedroom. Two mattresses were on the floor squeezed closely together. Two children played, a little boy and little Mim. The young girl was now wearing tattered clothing. She closed her eyes and they both collapsed on the mattress, seemingly unconscious. Isla gasped.

"It was a game for us, and we learned a lot about Somnium." The children awoke laughing.

The image faded and they were in the room with all the mirrors and doors. Mim had transformed back into an adult. "I eventually discovered that I could bring Marcu into my dreams, but I could also go into his if I chose. I learned that when I was in his dreams I couldn't change things, but when we were in mine I could. Marcu was different. When he was in my dream he could manipulate it just like he could in his own dream. He's what we call a dreamweaver."

The scene around them changed and they were now outside of a small building. Isla saw a little boy running around a middle-aged version of Mim. Next to them was a tall lanky man.

"Years later, when your father was little, we discovered he had a much different ability. As hard as I tried I couldn't enter his dreams and it wasn't long before I realized that when he was touching me I couldn't enter Somnium. It was then that Marcu," Mim gestured toward the man next to them, "convinced me to start a school with him. We would teach students with a connection to Somnium how to control their abilities."

"What happened to your brother? I've never heard Dad mention Uncle Marcu before."

"Marcu became obsessed with learning everything there is to know about Somnium, particularly where our abilities come from. Over time his interest in the school became less and less, until eventually he stopped teaching at all. A few years before you were born he left to try and find answers. Since then I've only seen him in Somnium, but lately I don't think he wants to be found," Mim said, forlorn.

Isla wasn't sure what to say next, it seemed best to change the subject. "How did you find students for your school?"

"Because I am a sandman, I can sense when someone is a theta—I can feel their connection to Somnium. Even though I can bring anyone I want with me, it's easier if they're a theta. Thetas accept the dream realm more readily than others."

"Are all thetas born with their abilities?" Isla asked.

"No, not everyone. Those of us who have an ability tend to pass that connection onto our children, but sometimes people can be taught." Mim paused. "When a theta doesn't know about their ability it can have devastating consequences on their life. Sometimes it can be very scary."

Isla thought back to her experience in Somnium the night before. "I can totally relate."

"I wanted to help people, and I knew there were thetas who were struggling. We originally put an ad in the paper to help people who were having trouble sleeping. I would meet with the applicants and those that I identified as thetas would go into a program to learn about Somnium. The others we referred to sleep disorder clinics, like your father's. The response to the ad was remarkable. We found more thetas than we expected and some of them had abilities that we weren't even aware existed."

Isla was about to ask about them, but stopped when Mim continued. "The school grew quickly as word spread among thetas. Your mother became one of our students as well…that's how your parents met. She was a sleepwalker like you. Do you want to see her?" Mim asked.

Isla nodded emphatically.

They were now in a small office that resembled a library. Every wall was lined with bookshelves that were completely full. It was the kind of place that Isla would love to cozy up in and read the day away. Isla tried to hold back her laughter when she spotted Mim with unusually long brown hair, no glasses, and unfashionably bright orange pants. Michael and Shayla were sitting on a couch holding hands. They both had huge grins.

"Shayla's going to have a baby," her father said, clearly unable to hold back his excitement. Mim clapped her hands and rushed to give them both a hug.

Shayla's smile grew bigger. "If it's a girl we're going to name her Isla. Since Miriam means 'lady of the sea' it only makes sense that your first grandchild be your 'island'."

Mim gasped at the thoughtful gesture as she pulled Shayla in for a bigger hug. Isla watched a tear drip below her grandmother's glasses.

Isla stepped forward into the scene, in awe of seeing her mother alive and moving. She reached out to try and touch her, but her hand passed right through like a mirage. Her eyes welled with tears. The memory faded and it was just Isla and Mim again.

Mim cleared her throat as she wiped her cheek. "Let's find out how strong your ability is, shall we?" her grandmother suggested.

Isla shrugged, not really sure what to do.

"Walkers are able to see Exsomnis and move around while staying asleep in Somnium. I want you to close your eyes."

Isla closed her eyes as instructed.

"Feel the park bench beneath you, feel the breeze on your cheeks," Mim said in a soft voice, as if trying to hypnotize her.

Isla thought about the park bench and the forest behind the Center and opened her eyes. To her surprise she was able to see Mim next to her with her eyes closed. She looked around and behind her found Mim with the floating orbs.

"This is weird," Isla said slowly.

"What do you see, dear?" Mim asked encouragingly.

"I'm sitting on the park bench and you're next me, still asleep."

"That's right," said Mim. "My consciousness is still in Somnium and yours is now somewhere between both. More precisely, in both. While you are now in both Somnium and Exsomnis and see both, I can still only see my dream in Somnium. So while you see the park bench, I cannot."

Isla was in complete disbelief.

"Look around for something small to pick up and then bring it to me," Mim said.

Isla saw a small flower with white petals on the ground. She bent over and picked it, then brought it to Mim as she requested.

"Lovely. Now, I want you to think about the flower melting," Mim said as Isla directed her eyes down at the flower.

Isla imagined the flower melting as Mim had instructed. The petals dripped like white paint sliding through her fingers.

Mim chuckled at Isla's amazed expression. "By bringing the flower back to me you brought the idea of it with you, because you can't actually bring it into Somnium. Since it was never in my mind, you control it. Does that make sense?"

"I think so."

Isla watched as the same white flower appeared in Mim's hands. Mim gave the flower to Isla and said, "Now try again."

Isla took the flower and imagined it melting again, but this time nothing happened. She tried harder and felt frustrated that it wasn't as easy as the first time.

"See, you can't control the flower now because I created it. Since we are in my version of Somnium, you can't control anything you don't bring in yourself. Now if Marcu or Rae were here, they could melt the flower so long as they were holding it. They are dreamweavers, so they can control things they touch in any dream they are in, even mine."

"Okay, I think I'm getting it." *Sort of*, she thought. "So is my body actually moving in Exsomnis?"

"It will when you choose to move," Mim said. "Your mind does an excellent job at melding the two realms together so that you aren't confused. You could even talk with someone in Exsomnis. You are as awake there as you are here."

"So how do I not bump into things in one realm or the other?"

"Your consciousness is active in both realms, so when you are walking you will be fully aware of everything around you in the dream and in Exsomnis. If there is an obstacle of some sort in either you will know it's there."

It was starting to make a little more sense to Isla. "What about when I talk?" she asked.

"You will be heard in both realms, but the person you are speaking to won't be heard on the other side. That's why sleepwalkers are so often misunderstood," Mim said. "It may seem as though they are talking nonsense to the person awake in Exsomnis."

"So how can I decide to be in one or the other?" she asked.

Mim ushered Isla to her side. "You are allowing your consciousness to be in both. All you must do is pull it in one direction, and as you do the other realm will fade." Isla concentrated on Mim's dream and to her delight she watched as the wall of frames and mirrors replaced the forest and park bench. Exsomnis was slowly fading away as Mim said it would.

"Now my dear, for you to learn the real power behind your ability. I want you to bring your consciousness to Exsomnis again but keep it in Somnium with me too."

Isla did as instructed and saw the park bench reappear.

"I want you to bring your consciousness all the way to Exsomnis and leave Somnium behind, but as you do you are going to bring me with you. Here, take my hand. When you hold one hand from each realm you are locking my consciousness in Somnium together with my body in Exsomnis."

Isla took her grandmother's hand in Somnium and walked them back over to the bench. "So I can do the same thing you can?"

"Not exactly, but it's similar. I can bring people in and out of Somnium by simply thinking about them. I don't need to be touching them, although it does help me if I am. In order for you to bring people in or out, you must be sleepwalking and you have to be touching them."

Isla still appeared perplexed, but she took Mim's hand in Exsomnis. "Okay, now what?"

"When our consciousness travels between Somnium and Exsomnis, we go through what we call the darkness. It allows our consciousness to transition from one realm to the other. When walkers travel between the two realms, you don't go through the darkness because you aren't fully asleep nor fully awake."

"Okay."

"You are holding my hand on the bench then?" Mim confirmed.

"Yes."

"You are going to focus only on Exsomnis. It will be like just a moment ago when you made Somnium fade away. As your consciousness travels fully to Exsomnis, so will mine."

Isla held onto both of Mim's hands.

"I am going to disappear with Somnium, but do not be afraid," Mim said knowingly.

Isla watched as Mim's dream began to fade the same way the forest had a few moments ago. Instead of the fabric overhead, she now saw the sky. She looked at Mim in Somnium, who was smiling encouragingly, and watched in awe as her grandmother turned translucent with everything else. As Somnium disappeared completely, so did Mim.

Next to Isla, Mim awoke. She pulled her granddaughter in for a hug. "You are a good student my dear, I'm so proud of you."

Isla timidly accepted the hug. This was all so new, and she wasn't sure she was ready for any of it.

CHAPTER 17

Michael and Rae stopped their conversation when Isla and Mim walked into Ethan's room at the Center. Rae stood up to leave. "I'm going to make up one of the spare beds to sleep in tonight—I want to be here in case there's anything I can do."

Michael gave Rae an appreciative smile before looking to Mim expectantly.

"Isla's going to be a skilled walker one day," Mim said with pride in her voice. "She was easily able to move between Somnium and Exsomnis."

Michael gave a small sigh of relief. "Would you mind giving us a few minutes?"

Mim nodded and quietly left the room.

Isla sat down in her favorite chair and squeezed her legs up to her chest. "I want to help Ethan," she said. "I need to help Ethan."

"I know you want to, honey."

Isla looked at her brother laying in his hospital bed and got up from the chair to go to his side. She grabbed Ethan's hand and decided it was time to confide her secret. "It's my fault he's trapped in Somnium."

Michael furrowed his brow in confusion.

Isla explained to her father how she had yelled at him and rushed him, causing him to fall off the swing. She covered her face as the guilt consumed her.

Michael got up and stood behind Isla. "This is not your fault," he said firmly. "It was an accident." He picked up one of his son's hands and then reached over for his daughter's, holding them both tightly. "We will get through this together. I have to believe that everything is going to turn out fine."

Isla spent the next few hours with Mim making small talk about their lives. Isla tried to stay focused, but her mind was still reeling from what she had learned that day. When it was time for her to go to bed Isla begrudgingly left her grandmother's side to put on her pajamas and brush her teeth. As she climbed into bed she implored her father, "Please Dad, is there nothing I can do to help?"

"I need to know you are both safe and the safest place for you tonight is sound asleep in your bed."

"And not dreaming," Isla added, looking disappointed. She grabbed her favorite blanket and curled up into a ball. "Good night, Dad."

Michael gave her a kiss on the forehead. "I love you so much," he said to her before he walked out of the room, closing the door gently behind him.

Isla rolled over and studied her brother. She remembered Mim's memory of playing with her brother Marcu and wondered if her and Ethan would ever have that kind of relationship.

Michael joined Dr. Prasad and his mother in his office to discuss Ethan's current state. Disappointment crossed Mim's face. "I've attempted to pull Ethan out, but it would appear it's not going to be as simple as that. As you suspected, his will to stay in Somnium seems to be too strong. He will need to be convinced that he's dreaming to break that connection."

Mim sat up straighter. "So this is the plan. Amit is going to observe the latest about Ethan's dream so that I am better prepared to enter Somnium and retrieve him. We know that Ethan has surrounded himself with a forest. That could make it more difficult for me to find the boy. Michael, do you have any ideas about how to navigate this forest?"

Michael sat back thoughtfully. "I think Ethan's scared and the forest has manifested itself from that fear. If that's the case, then I don't think he'll willingly leave the house. I'm quite certain that's where you'll find him."

Dr. Prasad nodded to Michael, indicating it was time to release his son from the darkness and rushed off to Ethan's room. A few minutes later he returned.

"Ethan is still inside the house, which is good. When you enter Somnium, go there. I believe he is currently alone. Get to him quickly and bring him back."

Mim closed her eyes. In her mind she focused on Ethan and everything went black as she entered the darkness. She opened her eyes in Somnium. In front of her was Ethan's house and around her was the forest that Dr. Prasad had described. She considered for a moment yelling to her grandson but thought that might frighten him. She decided perhaps it was best to do what would be expected in Exsomnis and knock on the door.

Mim took a few steps forward when all of a sudden everything changed. She stopped abruptly and looked around. She could no longer see the house—it was as if she had been transported somewhere else within the woods. Mim wandered around and was beginning to lose hope when she caught a glimpse of light reflecting off a window. She cautiously approached the house from the backside this time, but just like before when she got closer, she was transported somewhere else. It was as if she was purposefully being kept out of the house.

Mim was growing frustrated. If she couldn't get to the house she would need someone who had the ability to change the dream for her so that she could. She needed a weaver. Mim sighed and pulled herself through the darkness and awoke in Exsomnis. She opened her eyes and began to recount what had happened when she felt Dr. Prasad remove his hand from her arm.

"We know," he said.

"I can't seem to get through to the house on my own. I'm going to need the assistance of a weaver if I am to get to Ethan."

"Rae is still here. You can bring her in to weave for you."

Mim was hesitant. "She's so young and inexperienced though, surely you want someone more capable."

Michael stood resolute. "It should be Rae. Ethan knows her and will be more likely to trust her."

Mim was still unconvinced, but trusted her son's judgement.

"I'll go get her," said Dr. Prasad.

There was a knock at the door and Michael looked up to see Christopher standing there. "Christopher," Michael said. "It's your night off. Is everything okay?"

"Yes, of course sir. I just happened to be driving by and thought I'd stop in to review Ethan's results from last night again. You know…in case we might have missed something."

"That's thoughtful, but you don't need to go to the trouble."

"It's no trouble at all—anything I can do to help." Before Michael could respond, Christopher closed the door and disappeared.

CHAPTER 18

Ethan opened his eyes and found he was sitting at the kitchen table. He couldn't remember how he got there.

"Dad?" Ethan called out to the empty house. "Isla?" He wished they were with him.

He got up to go look for them when he saw Nox come around the corner.

"Hey kitty," he said as he patted the cat.

Ethan looked down the hall and saw movement coming from where the cat had been.

"I see you've met your new cat," he heard his father say.

"Dad!" Ethan said gleefully as he ran down the hall and threw his arms around his father, who lifted him up off the ground and held him tight.

"Wait...my cat?" he asked, his voice muffled by his father's chest.

"Of course. I know you've been taking such great care of Nox while we were gone. You've proven that you deserve to keep the cat. If Isla wants a pet of her own, she needs to prove she can be as responsible as you've been." Michael put Ethan down and gave his son a wink.

Isla came bounding around the corner and Ethan fought the urge to stick out his tongue at her.

"Where have you been?" Ethan demanded.

Isla gave her brother a shrug. "I'm sorry, Ethan. I know I shouldn't have left you here alone. I'll tell you what…let me make it up to you. You pick a game and I promise to play it."

Ethan wasn't sure that was a good idea. Playing games with her never ended well. She beamed at him and something about her expression felt disarming to Ethan. Still, he decided to push her buttons.

"Okay, how about Go Fish?" Ethan asked, knowing that was her least favorite game.

Isla's smile broadened. "Of course, Ethan. I did say I'd play *any* game you want."

Ethan cocked his head to the side and squinted at his sister. *What is she up to?* He wondered if their father was forcing Isla to be nice, but Michael seemed just as shocked by her attitude as Ethan.

"You better take her up on that offer while you still can," he said with a chuckle.

Ethan didn't wait another second lest Isla change her mind. He raced upstairs to search his closet for his lucky deck of cards. Of course they were nowhere to be found. He looked around the room thinking he really needed to clean it up and was shocked when the mess disappeared. He spun back to his organized closet. It was full of stuff, but none of it seemed quite like his. After moving some things around in the closet he gave up. Ethan walked downstairs feeling a little dejected.

"What's the matter?" Isla asked.

"I couldn't find the deck of cards."

Isla smiled and pulled her hands out from behind her back. "You mean *these* cards?" she asked with a mischievous glint in her eyes. Ethan giggled at her attempt to do magic.

She sat down at the kitchen table, shuffling the cards like a professional dealer. Ethan was mesmerized.

"Didn't I promise to teach you how to do this a long time ago?"

Ethan shrugged.

"Now's as good a time as any," she said.

For what felt like an hour they sat together, Isla giving Ethan helpful tips on how to shuffle. With each attempt he got better until finally he was doing it almost as well as Isla could.

"Dad, come quick, you have to see this!" Isla shouted.

Their father appeared in the kitchen. "It's so wonderful seeing you two get along so well."

Ethan smiled up at his father and then over at Isla. He just about fell over when she opened her arms for a hug. Ethan raised an eyebrow at her, but she opened her arms wider and he caved, rushing into her embrace. As much as he was loving the attention, it just didn't feel right.

Ethan slowly backed away and eyed his sister closely. "What's going on here?" he asked.

"I'm just showing you the love that you've always deserved."

Ethan narrowed his eyes. "Are you dying or something?" he asked his sister. "Am I dying?" He sucked in his breath and stared at his father. "Are you dying?"

Michael's expression was sympathetic. "No one's dying, buddy. You're just being treated the way you deserve."

Ethan raced over to his father and gave him a squeeze, concerned that maybe his father wasn't real and he was just imagining all of this. Isla joined in on the hug.

"I haven't been the best sister to you Ethan, but that's all going to change. From now on everything we do will be what you want. No more arguing, I promise. We'll be the best of friends."

Ethan stepped back from the group hug feeling a little puzzled. Like the house that was a little different, his father and Isla were different too.

Ethan looked down when he felt Nox rub against his leg. He picked up the cat and stroked its fur and decided maybe it was best to accept the new changes in them. After all, it *was* what he always wanted, for Isla to treat him even just a little bit better.

He dropped Nox to the floor and reached out a hand to his sister. "You've got to come check out the pool!"

A little while later, Ethan and Isla came racing up the stairs giggling, both of them still dripping from swimming in the basement. They slumped on the couch, out of breath.

"Dad's going to kill us if he finds us on the couch in these wet suits," Isla said.

Ethan knew she was right and thought how nice it would be if they were wearing dry clothes, but he didn't feel like getting back up. He proudly pointed at his sister's torso. Isla looked down at her sweatshirt and pants and then at Ethan's own dry clothes.

"Oh, cool. I don't even remember getting changed."

Ethan leaned forward a little bit. He was going to ask Isla what she wanted to do next, but he stopped when he figured she must be getting bored. His sister never spent this much time with him.

She noticed his apprehension. "What is it?"

"Nothing. It's just, well…I've had a lot of fun with you today, Isla."

"Me too, Ethan. We're going to have lots more days like this."

Nox meowed as it came around the corner, eyes glinting in the afternoon sun. Ethan bent down and picked up the cat. He looked over at his sister, who was eyeing his new pet. "Would you like to hold it?"

Isla eagerly reached her arms out to take the cat. Ethan handed over Nox, who snuggled into Isla's neck and purred loudly. Isla closed her eyes and nuzzled the soft fur.

Ethan eyed his sister curiously. It was as though she had been replaced by a different Isla, albeit a much nicer version. He wanted to accept this new reality, but there was a distant feeling in the back of his mind that kept telling him that something wasn't right.

Nox jumped out of Isla's arms and into Ethan's lap, as if sensing a change in the boy. Ethan patted the cat as he surveyed the room, trying to identify the things that were slightly different. The couch wasn't quite the right color, and the chair in the corner was the wrong shape. There were curtains on the windows where there should have been blinds, and outside the window was a forest when their house should be surrounded by other homes. *If only everything was as it should be.*

Nox raised a paw and tapped the side of Ethan's face. He laughed at the cat. "I'm sorry, was I ignoring you?" When he looked around the room again, the things that didn't seem right were all of a sudden back to normal. Ethan narrowed his eyes. Perhaps he had been imagining things.

"What's going on in here, kiddos?" Michael asked as he entered the living room. "It's gorgeous, why don't you go outside and play?"

Ethan peered out the window. The inside of the house may have changed, but outside the forest remained. "I'm not going out there."

Michael followed his son's gaze. "I know bud, ever since you got lost out there you've been scared to go out alone."

"That was at the Center, Dad."

"You must be confusing that with something else," his father said. "Don't you remember?"

Getting lost in the woods was something Ethan would never forget, of course he remembered.

"It was a scary day Ethan, for all of us. You shouldn't have gone outside alone," said Isla.

Ethan was starting to get angry that they weren't remembering correctly. He got lost in the woods behind the Center. He was sure of it. He needed them to believe him.

"Oh yes Ethan, of course you're right." His father shook his head as though it just occurred to him that he'd been wrong.

Ethan had the distinct feeling that this was some crazy weird dream. He thought about Isla standing up and doing a disco dance. To his amazement, Isla laughed and then stood up and began to dance.

Ethan eyed his sister suspiciously before he raced upstairs to her bedroom. He heard her running up the stairs behind him. Ethan threw open the door, Isla close on his heels. He braced for her to grab him and physically remove him from her room, but he felt her tickling his sides instead.

"You think you're funny, do you?" she asked, giggling.

Ethan shrieked with glee and wrapped his arms around her in a hug. This was the sister he always wanted Isla to be, but knew this must be a dream. He sighed, wanting to be alone. His arms fell to his sides as Isla disappeared. He sank down to the floor, squeezed his eyes shut tight and repeatedly told himself to wake up. Nothing happened.

He opened his eyes, feeling frustrated. He pinched his arm and kept squeezing harder and harder until tears were forming in his eyes. *Well*, thought Ethan, *if I'm not dreaming, where am I?*

CHAPTER 19

Rae walked uneasily into Michael's office. "It's nice to see you again, Mrs. Rosedale. I'm looking forward to returning to classes with you once my internship here at the Center is over."

"Please, call me Mim." She gestured for Rae to sit in the chair at her side.

When she was settled, Mim leaned back with her eyes closed. She focused on Ethan and the house as she passed through the darkness and into Somnium. Rae felt her vision start to black out and closed her eyes as well. Mim opened her eyes and found Rae grinning.

"Going into someone else's Somnium is such a rush," she breathed.

Mim looked around. There was no house and nothing around her was familiar. "Things must have changed again," she said, disappointed.

Rae thought for a moment, then she plucked a few small branches and leaves from the trees nearby. She molded them into what resembled a bird and whispered into its ear. Rae opened her hands and the leaf bird hopped out and flew up into the sky. Mim stepped back and admired the bird as it fluttered away.

"That's very clever, dear."

"Hopefully it'll just be a few minutes," Rae said. She watched intently through the bird's eyes as it flew above the forest. She clapped her hands when she saw the house and then had the leaf bird fly back to them. Upon returning, it circled them a few times and then headed for a path behind them.

They followed the bird, moving slower on foot. Rae wondered how much time had passed. Forgetting that watches stopped moving in Somnium, she glanced down at her wrist. As she did so, she walked into Mim by accident.

Rae blushed as the older woman motioned for her to stop where she was. The house was in front of them. "We have to stop here," Mim said. "If we go any further I'm sure that we'll get transported somewhere else and be back at square one."

Rae pointed to the leaf bird, which had landed on a branch just next to the house. "It looks like my little friend can get through," she said excitedly.

"I'm not sure how your bird is going to help us get to Ethan."

"The bird can bring Ethan to us," Rae said as she waved the leaf bird onward.

The leaf bird took off and flew to the house. It tapped its beak on the glass door leading into the kitchen. Ethan curiously approached the door and opened it to get a closer look at the leaf bird. The bird hopped around in excitement. Ethan followed its movements with an expression of amusement and joy.

"Where did you come from, little guy?"

Ethan knelt down to the little bird and tried to pat it. It wiggled under Ethan's touch and chirped loudly. It flew in a few circles around Ethan and then started to fly back towards the forest. The next thing Ethan knew, Nox came leaping out of nowhere and caught the leaf bird, shaking it until it had fallen apart. The cat dropped the remains at Ethan's feet and meowed with pride. Ethan frowned at the cat as he picked up the crushed leaves in the doorway and threw them outside.

Rae and Mim watched, dismayed. Rae took a few steps forward to try and yell to Ethan when she saw movement out of the corner of her eye. She turned to see what it was when she felt something come crashing across her face, causing her to fall to the ground.

Rae rolled over searching for what had hit her in the head. She eyed a branch that was still swinging and shrieked when she realized that the entire tree was moving as if it had feet of its own. She pulled herself to her knees and grabbed a handful of stones from the ground. She threw them in the air, forming netting between them as they began descending. The net captured the moving tree, causing it to flail. It crashed to the ground, its limbs broken and lifeless.

"Did Ethan do this?" Rae asked, breathing heavily.

Mim looked at the house where her grandson had disappeared back inside. "I don't think so."

Rae searched around them frantically, trying to find the dreamweaver that had made the tree come to life.

"There must be someone else here...a trespasser," Rae said.

"I'm not so sure. We need to regroup." Mim rushed over to Rae's side to help lift her up and bring her to Exsomnis. As Rae's vision began to fade to the darkness, she glanced back at the tree that had attacked her. She saw a black cat sitting nearby, watching them.

Isla opened her eyes and gaped at the forest she had seen in her dream the night before. Her heart began to race as she remembered the monster with the yellow eyes that seemed to be lurking whenever she dreamt. She slumped down on the ground and leaned against a tree, squeezing her eyes shut. She felt paralyzed by fear.

This is just a dream. I'm just dreaming. She repeated the mantra over and over again, but she didn't feel convinced. She opened her eyes and raised her arms in front of her, forming an "x" like Mim had shown her earlier and willed them to pass through each other. *I am dreaming*, she realized as they easily passed through each other.

Isla took a deep breath and remembered that she had control over her own dream. She sat back and imagined the trees shrinking so she could see the sky. Nothing happened. *I must not be doing this right.*

She looked down at the ground and found a small flower similar to the one she had plucked from outside the Center. She concentrated on turning it to liquid. Still, nothing happened.

Isla stood up, frustrated. It had been so easy with Mim earlier—why couldn't she change whatever she wanted now? She whirled around thinking about turning the leaves purple, the sky red, the ground to water. Isla let out a scream when nothing changed.

The forest felt like it was closing in around her.

She decided to bring her consciousness to the Center. She closed her eyes and focused on herself sleeping in the bed. When she opened them, she saw one of the chairs in the room start to appear through the forest. She tried harder and began to move her body in the room when she noticed Christopher hovering over her bed.

He must be checking on us.

"Christopher," she whispered. "Do you see the trees over there?" She gestured behind her at the wall. "I can't make them go away."

Christopher appeared shocked to see her awake. "Shhh," he said. "It's all right, Isla."

"But the trees, Christopher…"

"There are no trees, Isla. You're just dreaming."

Isla felt even more frustrated and she sat up, attempting to get out of the bed. As she stood, her knees buckled and she fell to the floor. She felt weak.

Christopher rushed over and scooped her up, placing her in the bed. "There there, now," he said. "It's time to go back to sleep."

"I'm not sleeping," she insisted. "I need to get out of bed."

She tried to sit up again, but the room spun around her and she collapsed onto the bed.

"Isla, you're just confused," he said as he took her hand.

With that, Exsomnis disappeared and Isla was in the forest alone. No matter how hard she tried she couldn't bring her consciousness to the Center.

She angrily kicked the dirt under her feet, immediately regretting it when she stubbed her toe. She looked down at her bare feet and pajamas before grabbing her foot. Once the pain subsided she picked another flower and sat on a patch of grass. She held it in her fingers, willing it to turn to liquid. She tried as hard as she could, but it still wasn't working.

Maybe it worked earlier because the flower had come from Exsomnis, she thought. She focused again on the hospital room, still feeling groggy. There was something soft under her hand, her favorite blanket. She clutched it firmly. When she opened her eyes, she was in Somnium holding her blanket. She held onto both ends and imagined it floating into the sky like a parachute. To her amazement, it worked. She gripped the blanket as it floated up above the trees. She drifted back down to the ground and plucked yet another flower. No matter how hard she tried, she still couldn't turn it to liquid.

Isla's stomach dropped as she came to the terrifying realization that this must not be her own dream. *Where am I?*

Isla wrapped the blanket around her body, hoping it would bring her some comfort. Maybe if she sat still long enough she'd wake up again. On second thought, perhaps the best thing she could do was figure out whose dream she was in. It was better than sitting still waiting for the monster to find her.

Isla stood up and fanned out her blanket. She figured if she could get up high enough into the sky maybe she would see someone else. At the very least, she wouldn't be walking around barefoot. She imagined her blanket had loops she could use to secure her hands. She grinned as she watched the blanket change to her will.

Isla placed her hands through the loops, readied herself, and ascended up above the trees. She saw what appeared to be a house in the middle of the forest. *Maybe I'll find someone there*, she thought.

CHAPTER 20

Rae's eyes flew open and she instinctively jumped up from her chair.

"You were attacked?" Michael asked when Rae and Mim awoke, clearly perturbed.

"I think you're right. There must be someone else in Ethan's dream. If you don't believe it was a trespasser, who do you think it was?" Dr. Prasad asked, looking at Mim.

"It doesn't make sense," she said. "Someone needed to touch the tree to control it, but I didn't see anyone else there."

"I didn't think it could be possible," Michael said quietly. "But Shayla said Iteiri would try to use the children. I dismissed it because it sounded crazy, but do you think it might actually be true?"

"Iteiri?" Rae asked. "What are Iteiri?"

"The Iteiri…" Mim started and then trailed off. It was a statement and a question at the same time. Mim shook her head in disbelief. "There is an ancient legend that tells of a tribe of people known as the Iteiri. It is said that the entire tribe were people of the night, what we now call thetas. They preferred to live in their dreams, choosing to control the world around them. They would wake long enough to care for their human bodies and assist the tribe before their leader, a sandman called Amani, would return them to Somnium. Due to the amount of time they spent in Somnium their abilities were strong, perhaps stronger than any that exist today."

Mim stood and began to pace.

"They were not fighters, so when intruders neared the tribe Amani would bring them into Somnium. Other members of the tribe would then weave nightmares to scare them. The Iteiri would show them visions of their deaths if they proceeded any further. The intruders would awake terrified and retreat. Eventually word spread of this tribe that could induce nightmares. Their peaceful lives took a very dark turn as others became afraid of what else the Iteiri could do to them as they slept."

"It is said that a huge army was amassed to attack the Iteiri. There were so many that Amani was unable to bring them all into Somnium. The army massacred the entire tribe, killing all of the Iteiri as they slept. The legend says that they now wander Somnium unseen, their consciousnesses trapped for eternity."

Michael inhaled deeply. "This is just an old story, it can't possibly be true."

"Most legends have some basis in reality," said Dr. Prasad. "We all know there are things in Somnium that we can't explain—perhaps this is why."

"If Shayla was right, how do we protect the children from something we can't see?"

"We need to get Ethan to wake, but we can't get to the house. It makes no sense—I've seen the dream now. We should be placed directly in the house, but each time I've tried we have ended up in the forest."

Dr. Prasad jumped up from his chair. "I understand now," he said. "When you try to go to the house you end up in the forest, no?"

"Yes, that's right."

"In Ethan's dream there is a forest in place of Michael's office. I believe that must be where you are when you enter Somnium. You are in the office but it's masking the house around it. Rae should be able to weave an opening if you can find the doorway."

Mim considered the idea. *That might explain why we aren't able to get through to the house, but it doesn't make our job any easier,* she thought.

With Rae's hand on her arm, Mim leaned back in her chair, focusing on the house they had seen in Somnium and pulled them both there. As she expected, when she opened her eyes the two of them were standing in the forest.

Mim looked around thoughtfully. "If Amit is correct, then we are in the house. So, how do we find the doorway?"

"Let me try something," Rae said. She reached down and picked up a pinecone. It grew arms and legs in Rae's hands. She gently placed it down on the ground and closed her eyes. The little pinecone man multiplied into an army. Rae opened her eyes and ordered the pinecone men to form a circle around the women. She then sent them marching away.

They watched the pinecone men intently when suddenly there was a flash of light forcing them to close their eyes. When they opened them again, some of the pinecone men were gone, the rest still marching onward.

"Brilliant—now we know exactly where the doorway is," said Mim.

"Let me try and weave it open like Dr. Prasad suggested."

Rae walked as close to the entrance as she dared and reached out her hand, hoping some part of her was touching the doorway. She focused all of her energy on creating an opening so they could see the house. She was delighted when she saw the main hallway of the house through a small hole around her wrist. It wasn't long before it was large enough for them to step through. "Ready?"

"You go first," said Mim. "If there's a chance it closes before we can both get through, Ethan will recognize you. If that happens you must bring him back to this spot as quickly as possible. He needs to believe he's dreaming so I can get us all to Exsomnis. Understood?"

Rae nodded and the two of them lined up in front of the opening. They stepped forward. When Rae reached the doorway she was blinded by the big flash of light but kept walking, hoping her plan had worked. When she opened her eyes again she gave a little "whoop" of excitement that she had made it through.

Rae's delight quickly faded when she looked for Mim and discovered she was alone. She waited for a few minutes and saw Mim reappear where they had started.

Rae waved at Mim, but she could tell from the look on the woman's face that she wasn't seeing into the house. She stepped closer to the doorway without crossing through and extended her hand until a small opening began to form at her fingertips.

"There's no time for that," Mim said through the hole when she saw Rae. "Just go find Ethan."

Rae didn't like the idea of splitting up but wasn't about to argue. She removed her hand from the doorway and the hole immediately closed.

The house was silent. Rae opened her mouth to yell for Ethan but thought better of it. If there was an Iteiri in Somnium with them it was probably best not to alert it of her presence. She quickly ran upstairs and checked all the bedrooms, but Ethan wasn't there. She ran downstairs to the kitchen and saw movement from behind the table.

"Ethan?" she asked softly. He didn't move. She came around the table and gently touched his arm. She jumped a little as he picked up his head and the cat in his lap became visible. His expression was blank as he methodically pet the cat, back and forth.

"Nurse Rae? What are you doing here? I didn't think about you."

"Well, I'm here to bring you home, honey. You're dreaming and I'm here to help you wake up." She looked around the room and saw a stuffed bear lying on the table. Rae placed the bear on the floor and directed it to walk towards Ethan and give him a hug.

Ethan didn't seem surprised to see the toy moving. He grabbed it and sent it marching back to Rae. Rae took the bear and examined Ethan's face. "Do you know you're dreaming?"

Ethan shrugged, as though he weren't quite sure. "If I'm dreaming why can't I wake up?"

"Your grandmother can help you wake up. We just have to go to her."

Rae reached out her hand to Ethan but he didn't take it.

"You're not real. We never see my grandmother, she wouldn't be here with you." Ethan rocked a little and put his hands on his head. "This is just all in my head. I want you to leave now." The boy turned away and Rae watched as he enclosed himself in a box. This wasn't working. If Ethan wouldn't willingly come with her she'd have to get Mim.

She ran out of the kitchen and down the hall towards the forest. Before she could step through the doorway she felt a sharp pain to the back of her head. As she fell to the ground, she looked up toward the ceiling. She felt another sharp pain to the side of her head as the darkness enveloped her and her consciousness slipped from Somnium.

Rae awoke with a start. She placed a hand to her head, half expecting to find blood, but in Exsomnis she remained unharmed. Dr. Prasad lifted his hand off of Rae as he was pulled from Somnium with her.

Rae's eyes darted around Michael's office. She was relieved when she saw Mim in the chair next to her, still asleep. Rae slowly stood up, trying to figure out what had happened. A pained expression crossed her face. "I was so close."

"I saw what happened Rae, there was nothing you could have done," said Dr. Prasad.

Rae was in shock. "Something must have killed me to force me out of Ethan's dream, but I saw nothing. Could there really be people in Somnium controlling things that we can't see?"

"You better check on her," Michael said to Dr. Prasad, gesturing at his mother.

Dr. Prasad placed a hand on her shoulder and his eyes began to flicker. "Miriam is fine. She's still standing in the forest, keeping an eye on the area you passed through. I can feel her apprehension. She's worried that you haven't returned. We should bring her back to Exsomnis."

Michael's eyes turned black as he pulled his mother's consciousness to the darkness, knowing that she would understand he was trying to wake her up.

Mim opened her eyes, appearing baffled.

Michael gestured to Rae, who was now standing before the older woman. "Something killed Rae... something she didn't see. I'm growing more and more anxious of Shayla's warning."

If Iteiri were in Ethan's dream, Michael wondered if they were also after Isla. His eyes became black as he frantically searched for his daughter in the darkness, but she wasn't there. His face drained of color when he felt her consciousness active in Somnium.

"Isla's...dreaming," Michael said, straining to get the words out. He jumped up and ran to Ethan's room, the others close behind.

Dr. Prasad stepped in front of Michael and placed a hand on Isla, his eyes flickering. "She's definitely in Somnium. She's floating above a forest and seems to be heading in the direction of a house...the house in Ethan's dream."

Michael sunk down, defeated. "I have to bring them to the darkness." He focused first on Isla, placing his hands on her arm. When nothing happened, he brought his attention to Ethan. His stomach dropped when he failed to bring either back.

"Why aren't I strong enough to pull them out?" Michael felt like a weight was crushing down on him.

"If there truly are Iteiri and Amani is real, well... wouldn't she be a very strong sandman?" asked Dr. Prasad.

"If there are beings stronger than all of us in Ethan's dream than what hope do we possibly have of helping the children?" Michael asked defeatedly.

Mim was thoughtful. "Aside from holding them in Somnium, the Iteiri don't seem to be harming the children. Shayla may have been right...maybe they need something from them. Rae and I will go back. If nothing else, we will be there to help protect the children. Perhaps if we can weaken Ethan's bond with Somnium we can break whatever hold the Iteiri have over him."

"Ethan is very confused. I don't think he can tell the difference between Somnium and Exsomnis," said Rae.

"Perhaps Isla will be able to convince him he's dreaming so we can get them out of there," Mim suggested.

Dr. Prasad placed his hand on Isla and his eyes flickered. "She's still floating towards the house. She should be easy to find." He removed his hand from Isla and walked over to the edge of Ethan's bed.

Rae wrapped an arm around Michael and gave it a soft squeeze. "We won't give up."

Michael grasped the young woman's hand. "I know you won't."

Mim surveyed the cramped room. "There isn't enough space in here for all of us. Rae and I will go back to your office. If you need us you know what to do," Mim said to her son.

Michael gave them a small smile as they left the room. He then pulled up a chair between his children, grabbing a hand from each of them. Dr. Prasad reached out to put a hand on Ethan when Michael spoke. "Please," he said, with tears in his eyes. "Don't tell me what's happening. Just let me know if there's anything I can do."

Dr. Prasad nodded his acknowledgement before his eyes began to flicker again as he watched what was unfolding.

CHAPTER 21

Ethan peered out the living room window. Dr. Prasad felt the boy's amazement when he saw a huge bird flying in the sky. As it got closer, he realized it was a person.

How on Earth? Ethan wondered. He squinted and Dr. Prasad saw that the person had a parachute.

Ethan was about to open the front door when Nox rubbed up against his leg. The cat jumped into a pile of presents in colorful wrapping paper in the middle of the room and Ethan's interest in the person outside quickly faded. It was like Christmas morning and he felt a rush of excitement, wondering what treasures could be inside the packages. He lifted a few, shaking them and trying to guess at the contents. He finally settled on the biggest gift in the pile and started ripping into the paper.

Each gift Ethan picked up he examined, thinking for a moment about what he wanted it to be. Before tearing into the paper he would quietly say the contents out loud.

"A bike."

"A new video game."

"A soccer ball."

"A watch."

"A phone."

Ethan quickly had an enormous pile of opened gifts. Dr. Prasad noticed that the pile wasn't getting any smaller. Ethan seemed to realize it too as he stopped, feeling almost disappointed. Somehow opening gifts wasn't so much fun when you knew exactly what you were getting.

The person parachuting around in the sky caught his attention again. He went to the window to look.

The parachute was the same shade of pink as his sister's favorite blanket.

"Isla?" he whispered.

Nox jumped up in the windowsill and began purring. Ethan began to absentmindedly pat the cat and Dr. Prasad could feel Ethan's attention to anything but the cat disappear. It was as if the animal had some sort of mind-numbing effect on the boy.

Dr. Prasad felt the cat's soft fur as Ethan repeatedly stroked it, back and forth. Ethan's mind went blank and for a long time he just stood there.

The boy's attention returned when Nox jumped out of the windowsill and ran straight for the forest in his father's office.

"Not again," Ethan groaned as he chased after the cat.

Ethan stopped in the doorway. He grabbed his backpack and was about to take off into the forest after Nox when he stopped abruptly.

He went back to the living room. Dr. Prasad sensed his disappointment that the pile of unopened gifts were gone. He didn't want his party to be over, even if no one else was there. His attention was brought to the ceiling as a disco ball began spinning around, casting a rainbow of colors all over the room.

Dr. Prasad heard music begin thumping throughout the house and watched as Ethan started to dance and sing along. Ethan glanced up at the disco ball, trying to remember what he had been doing.

"Isla." He rushed over to the window, but she was gone. Ethan spun around and found the gifts neatly packed away in boxes. Dr. Prasad could feel Ethan's irritation, assuming his sister had been the one to clean up his new toys.

Where could she have gone? he wondered.

A loud noise behind him made Ethan turn around. Nox had knocked over a family portrait, causing it to shatter on the floor.

"Oh no," he said as he picked up what was left of the frame. He flipped it over to see what damage had been done to the picture and his heart sank when he saw a big scratch across his sister's face.

"I have to fix this before Dad gets home. I'm going to need some glue."

Ethan collected the shards and began assembling them like puzzle pieces, carefully gluing them together as if they had never been broken in the first place. He finished repairing the frame and put the photograph back inside. He flipped it around and placed it on the mantle.

Good as new. Now…what was I supposed to do? he wondered. At his feet, Nox meowed.

"Hey kitty, you must be hungry." Ethan had the distinct feeling he was forgetting something. He looked around hoping it would jar his memory but when nothing came to mind he headed for the kitchen, the cat happily padding along at his side.

Mim and Rae settled into the large leather chairs in Michael's office. Mim nodded, indicating she was ready to take them both to Ethan's dream. Before she could, Rae reached out a hand to stop her.

"Do you really think we stand a chance?" Rae asked.

Mim's expression was not as hopeful as Rae had expected.

"I'm not sure," Mim said, looking off into the distance as she got lost in her thoughts.

"What do we do?" Rae asked. Mim's lack of confidence made the young nurse's blood run cold.

Mim brought her attention to Rae. "I'm afraid I don't know. Until tonight I thought the legend of the Iteiri was nothing more than a story to explain where nightmares come from. I never imagined they could actually be real."

Rae leaned back in her chair briefly and then sat up straight. "The Iteiri we encountered…it was like me. It changed Ethan's dream."

Mim gave Rae an encouraging nod to continue.

"In the story you told, you said Iteiri were thetas. If that's true, the one we encountered would be a dreamweaver. It must have had to touch the tree to control it, like I would. Perhaps we can't see them, but maybe their abilities work just like ours. So if I cast a wider net next time…"

"You could trap it," Mim finished.

Rae closed her eyes. She didn't feel ready, but she knew she had to be. They at least needed to stay alive long enough to get to Isla.

Mim gave Rae a soft pat on her knee and settled into her chair. When she opened her eyes she was standing next to Rae in the forest. "If their abilities are like ours, we'll have limited time before a sandman senses our presence."

Rae cautiously searched for anything that might attack them and then glanced up into the sky. She jumped when she saw Isla.

"Isla!" Rae yelled. Her hopes for easily retrieving the girl were quickly dashed when she realized Isla couldn't hear her.

"I can't get us up there," Mim said sadly. "We'll just fall to the ground. We'll need parachutes of our own."

Rae spun around, searching the forest for something she could use to serve as a parachute like Isla's. She began to feel anxious as her mind went blank, equal parts terrified and ashamed that her imagination was failing them.

"It's okay, my dear," Mim said sympathetically.

"It's not okay though," Rae said through tears. "Isla needs us and I'm down here failing." Rae glanced up at Isla, who was now further away.

"You can do this," Mim assured her.

Rae took a deep inhale and wiped away her tears, knowing she needed to figure this out quickly before the girl was completely out of their sight. A tree branch swaying in the breeze caught her attention. It had a large canopy of leaves and bowed in a perfect arch. Rae grabbed ahold of it, willing it to remove itself from the tree. She took it over to Mim, feeling satisfied. "This will do."

Mim smiled as she took the branch. Rae looked around and found a vine growing up another tree. She grabbed a handful and watched as it unwound itself from the tree. She used it to create a harness, turning the branch Mim was holding into a hang glider.

Rae made quick work of creating a second glider and climbed into the harness next to Mim. "Ready?" she asked.

"Ready," said Mim.

Rae willed the two hang gliders to raise up into the air. They ascended a few feet and then jerked to a stop. Rae's stomach dropped, fearing to look down at what had stopped them. She gasped when she saw that the vines from the harness were firmly planted in the ground. Something was trying to take control of the vines.

"The Iteiri is here," said Rae, her eyes wide.

She grabbed ahold of the vines on each harness and closed her eyes, trying to regain control. She shook her head, terrified. "I can't control both vines, it's too strong."

Rae watched in horror as the vine began to creep up her arms. She turned to Mim and was grateful to see that her arms remained free. The Iteiri was stronger than she was, but maybe not if she focused all her energy on one vine.

She quickly reached over and placed both hands on Mim's harness and willed it to turn to dust. She heaved a sigh of relief when Mim fell to the ground. She then grabbed onto her own harness before the Iteiri had a chance to realize what had happened. She sent the vine swirling in large sweeping circles, capturing the Iteiri within. She then broke the vine in dozens of places. In order to get out it would have to touch each piece individually.

Rae knew she wasn't going to be able to hold it for long. "You have to go get Isla's attention somehow," she said to Mim. "I'll keep it here as long as I can."

Before Mim disappeared completely she said, "I'll come back for you."

CHAPTER 22

Isla was feeling dejected. When it hadn't seemed like the house was getting much closer she had willed her parachute to lower down to the ground to give her arms a chance to rest.

When she looked up she was grateful to see someone waving at her. She squinted to try and get a better look, but the person was too far away to make out who it was.

She imagined the blanket turning into a small handkerchief and stuffed it into her pocket, figuring it may come in handy again. As the person got closer she recognized Mim's short gray hair. She rushed over to Mim and wrapped her arms around her tightly.

"I'm so glad you're here. I've been so scared," Isla said.

Mim squeezed her back, releasing her briskly. "We must move, and quickly. I've come to take you to Ethan."

"Is this Ethan's dream?"

"I'm afraid so," said Mim.

"I've been trying to bring myself to Exsomnis like you showed me, but I can't."

"I'm so sorry dear, but you can't leave yet."

Isla furrowed her brow at her grandmother. "Why not?"

Mim was quiet as she considered what to tell Isla. "Ethan needs you. I'm afraid he's unsure about whether or not he's awake. We can't wake him up if he doesn't believe."

"I'm not sure I understand what you're saying."

"There is more going on here than just a dream, Isla. Something very powerful is keeping you both in Somnium. I'm afraid the only way to break that hold is to make Ethan take back control of his dream. You need to convince him he's dreaming before it's too late."

The comfort that Isla had felt at seeing Mim was quickly fading away. "How am I supposed to do that? I can't control anything here."

Mim caressed Isla's arm. "You're his sister dear, that bond is stronger than you know."

Isla wasn't so sure Mim understood her relationship with her brother. Considering how things had gone the day of the accident, Isla was pretty sure Ethan wouldn't trust her at all.

"I can bring you to Ethan. Are you ready?"

She wasn't, but she slowly nodded her head yes.

The next thing Isla knew, they were standing elsewhere in the forest. Mim searched the trees and then pointed in front of them. "There. I know it doesn't look like much, but that is a doorway to your father's office."

Mim remembered the parachute Isla had been using and pointed to Isla's pocket.

"The handkerchief in your pocket, that's from Exsomnis?"

"Yes."

"I need you to turn that into a door right here." Mim walked forward and stopped short of the entrance. She bent over and drew a line in the dirt. "As it's changing, imagine it being a doorway that goes into the house."

Isla laid the handkerchief on top of the line and pictured it was a doorway like the one in her house. She watched in amazement as the small piece of fabric grew taller and taller as it changed into a wooden door. It looked terribly out of place between the trees.

"Quickly now," Mim said, ushering her to the door. "When you get on the other side, take the door with you. You may need something you can control again."

"You aren't coming with me?" Isla asked, agitated.

"Rae is here and she's in trouble. She needs my help."

Isla froze. She had just found someone she trusted to help her in an unfamiliar place and now she was about to be on her own again.

"Convince Ethan he's dreaming, and I may be able to bring us all back to Exsomnis."

Reluctantly Isla walked towards the door. She stopped before opening it. "How do I do that?"

"Just be his sister. You are exactly what he needs right now."

Isla reached out, opened the door, and stepped inside. The house was surprisingly similar to their house, but it was different in subtle ways. She saw the entrance to the forest in what should have been her father's office. "Take the door with you," Isla heard Mim say as she shut the door completely.

Isla imagined the door was a handkerchief again. When it was completely shrunk down, she picked it up and put it in her pocket.

Isla didn't waste another second before she began racing around the house looking for her brother. "Ethan," she kept saying as she rounded every corner. She checked all of the rooms on the first floor and then darted down to the basement. She stopped in awe when she saw the pool, but when it became clear her brother wasn't there she ran back up the stairs.

"Ethan!" she yelled. She was beginning to feel annoyed. *Why isn't he answering?*

Isla was reminded of the day of the accident and suddenly the weight of her guilt was upon her. *This isn't Ethan's fault,* she reminded herself.

She ran upstairs hoping to find him in his room, but he wasn't there. Her father's room was also empty. She ran down the hallway to her room thinking maybe he was messing with her, but he wasn't there either.

Isla sank down onto her bed feeling hopeless. If Ethan wasn't in the house, that meant he was outside, and she knew if he was out in the forest there was no way she was going to find him. Isla curled up into a ball, feeling like a complete failure.

How am I supposed to tell Mim that I couldn't even find Ethan? Isla needed her father, he always knew what to do. She wondered if she'd be able to return to Exsomnis now.

Isla shut her eyes and visualized the Center. When she opened her eyes, in front of her was her not-quite-right bedroom, but to her right she saw her father. She realized she was holding his hand. She gave it a soft squeeze.

"Dad," she said, feeling reassured.

Michael looked up at his daughter in shock. "Isla. Oh, thank goodness."

"I don't know what's going on Dad. Mim brought me to find Ethan, but now she's gone."

Michael eyed his daughter intently. "Are you sleepwalking?"

"Yes. I'm still in Somnium."

"Are you with Ethan?"

"No, I can't find him. Should I keep trying?"

"No, it's not safe for you to be there. You need to pull yourself to Exsomnis like Mim showed you."

Isla focused on the Center, but no matter how hard she tried, the bedroom in Somnium wasn't disappearing. "It's not working."

Michael was clearly disappointed.

"It's okay, Dad. Mim told me I need to convince Ethan he's dreaming. I want to stay and help...I'm just not sure how."

Dr. Prasad removed his hand from Ethan. "I don't think Ethan realizes that he's the one changing things in Somnium. It seems that each time he questions what's going on, he gets distracted by the cat in his dream. You need to get him away from the cat."

"How do I even find him though?"

Dr. Prasad placed his hand on Ethan and Isla watched in amazement as the doctor's eyes flickered. "Is he…"

"Watching Ethan's dream? Yes," Michael finished.

Isla thought about Jackson knowing details of her dream earlier that day and wondered if he was like Dr. Prasad.

"He's still in the house, Isla," said the doctor, bringing her attention back. "He's in a tiny room I've never seen. It almost looks like he's hiding."

"How am I supposed to find a hidden room?"

Dr. Prasad didn't answer, his eyes were darting all around the room. "There's a doorway. I can see the upstairs hallway through a small crack. Try looking again."

"You don't need to do this alone Isla," said her father. "You can continue sleepwalking through the house."

"I don't think I can do that Dad, although I'd much rather have you with me." She laid down on the bed.

Michael placed his hand on her arm to stop her. He pulled a pocketknife from his pants and put it into her hand. "Put this in your pocket."

Isla did as she was told and placed the knife into her pajama pants.

"Listen carefully to me," Michael said. "I'm afraid things could get dangerous. If they do, try to pull yourself back here. If that doesn't work, use the knife."

CHAPTER 23

Isla reluctantly let go of everything in Exsomnis except for her father's hand. As she did so, the Center faded away and she was alone again in her strange bedroom in Somnium.

As much as she wanted to give up right now, she knew the only way to make this right was to find Ethan. She walked out of her room and down the hallway but stopped quickly when she found a tiny door that didn't exist in their house.

How did I not see that before? Isla stepped inside the small room. It was empty.

Isla was about to leave and search elsewhere when she felt something. She wasn't sure what it was, but it made her want to stay.

"Ethan?" Isla asked quietly.

Her brother materialized out of nowhere. "Isla?" He tilted his head to the side, looking her over like he didn't recognize who she was.

Isla wondered what was going on in his head. "Ethan," she said as she ran over to him and grabbed his hands. "I need you to listen closely to me."

Ethan stared up at her. His eyes were exhausted, which seemed strange for someone who had been asleep for so long.

"Ethan, this is a dream."

He stared at Isla as though he wasn't hearing a word she said. He broke her gaze when he felt something on his leg.

"Nox," he said as he bent down to pick up the cat. The black cat purred as it peered at Isla with its yellow eyes.

Isla scowled at the cat. The thing made her feel uneasy.

"Ethan, that cat doesn't belong here," she said as she tried to push the animal out of his arms.

Ethan turned away angrily. "You always want what's mine, Isla, but you can't have the cat. Nox is mine. Dad said so."

Isla felt helpless. She didn't know how to make Ethan understand. She thought about her lesson with Mim. She wondered if she'd be able to pull Ethan to Exsomnis even though she couldn't pull herself through. She could tell that getting him to hold her hand was going to be a challenge.

Ethan walked past Isla and out of the room. She kept her distance as she followed him down the stairs. The cat crawled up on Ethan's shoulders and Isla swore it was grinning.

Ethan took the cat into the kitchen and placed an empty bowl on the floor, then sat down next to it. The next thing she knew, the bowl was full of cat food that came from nowhere. Nox munched happily on the food while Ethan patted the cat's back.

Isla decided to try a different approach. She sat down next to Ethan and stared at him intently. "Ethan, I'm sorry you're upset with me. You have every right to be."

The sincerity in her voice caught him off guard.

Nox sensed the change in Ethan's interest and cried out for his attention.

Ethan distractedly started patting the cat. "Now, now Nox. I need to listen," he said.

Isla raised an eyebrow at her brother. It seemed like he was under some kind of spell. Isla tried to think of some way to get her brother away from Nox when her hand brushed past the knife her father had given her earlier.

"Ethan…I need you to know that I love you. I would never want to hurt you on purpose. I really hope you understand that."

Ethan ignored her as he continued to pat Nox.

Isla inhaled deeply as she pulled the knife out of her pocket and stabbed it into the cat's side. Nox howled in pain. Isla gasped when no blood poured from the wound —it just looked like an empty hole. The creature stopped moving and crumpled to the ground. Nothing remained of Nox but velvet fabric and two gold coins.

Ethan began to scream as he scrambled to get away from the magician's cloak, his confusion apparent.

Isla saw her opportunity. She grabbed Ethan's hand and pulled him towards the kitchen door so they could escape into the forest. As Isla stepped outside Ethan pulled away, refusing to leave the house.

"Ethan, please. I need you to trust me."

Ethan's eyes appeared to be a little clearer. Isla took his silence as agreement and she pulled at his hand again. He yanked his hand back and ran down the hallway. To her surprise, he returned wearing a backpack.

Ethan grabbed his sister's hand. Without another word they ran into the forest. Isla didn't know where she was going, but since Mim was nowhere in sight she knew they had to quickly find a safe place. Isla saw a hedge of bushes and shoved Ethan into them, pulling him down so they were at least somewhat hidden.

"Ethan, you need to listen. We are inside your dream. That means you can control it. You need to do something to protect us."

"Isla, you're not making any sense. Look." He pinched his arm until it was bright pink.

Isla grabbed the backpack and began rummaging through it. It was filled with emergency supplies. She pulled out a can of bug repellent and sprayed it all over. Ethan began coughing through the mist.

"Make this hide us," Isla said, as she too wheezed through the heavily scented repellent.

Ethan looked at his sister like she was insane. She could tell that this wasn't going to work.

Isla reached into her pocket and pulled out the handkerchief. She imagined it was a camouflage blanket, then threw it over the two of them.

Not a moment later, the cat came scampering by, only now it looked like Ethan's magician's cloak. Isla motioned to Ethan as she put a finger to her lips. The cat's golden coin eyes glinted in their direction, but to Isla's relief it didn't seem to see them. It soon ran off.

"Isla, I'm scared," Ethan whimpered.

"I know Ethan, I'm scared too." She squeezed his hand.

Ethan huddled in tighter to his sister. "I don't think I can move."

Isla threw her arms around him. "Maybe you don't have to," she said as she pulled him in closer. "Do you trust me?"

Isla felt his head bob up and down on her shoulder. Isla closed her eyes and visualized the Center. She opened her eyes and saw her father. "I have Ethan."

"Take my hand," she said to her brother.

Her father's face was concerned.

"Dad, I stabbed the cat and it just collapsed into a pile of fabric."

"And that man that appeared out of nowhere..." Ethan said, astonished.

Isla was bewildered. "Dad, Ethan says he saw a man appear, but I didn't see that."

Dr. Prasad, who was still watching through Ethan's eyes said, "Yes, I saw the man too."

Michael's face turned white. He quickly stood up and wheeled Isla's bed close enough so that she could reach Ethan's hand in Exsomnis.

Isla grabbed her brother's small limp hand on the hospital bed and focused on the Center until bits of the forest began to fade. She looked over at Ethan, hoping she might be able to pull him through. Isla held her breath and gritted her teeth, trying to force Ethan to Exsomnis. No matter how hard she tried, she couldn't manage to pull him out. Her head was starting to hurt.

"I'm so sorry Dad," she said, defeated. "I can't."

"It's not your fault, honey."

"What do I do now? We can't stay here Dad."

"You need to find Mim, maybe she can help."

"Dad, I don't know if I can. We're lost out in the woods and Ethan just seems so confused."

"Isla, you do know that Dad isn't here, right?" Ethan asked his sister as if she were crazy.

Isla stared pleadingly at her father. Michael remained silent, feeling helpless.

"Mim is right. You must convince him," Dr. Prasad said.

"I'll try," she said as she let Exsomnis fade away.

Ethan was still looking at his sister like she had gone mad. Isla took a deep breath. "Ethan, I know you don't believe me, but I promise you that we're in your dream. We saw your cat collapse to the floor and it was just your cloak. You said yourself that you saw a man appear out of nowhere." She shuddered at the idea.

"Weird things have been happening all day Isla, if one of us is losing it here, it's you." Ethan put a pointed finger up to his ear and spun it around.

Isla was getting irritated. *How am I supposed to convince him of something he doesn't want to believe?*

"Ethan," she said sternly. "Don't you think it's time we go see Dad?"

"Yeah, where is he?"

Isla smiled softly. "He's at the Center. We're all at the Center. If you concentrate really hard maybe you can bring us there."

"Okay," he said easily. Before Isla could say another word, they were standing in the entryway to the Center.

Isla looked around in alarm, not sure how they had gotten there. She ran through the doors to the nurses' station. She was disappointed when she realized there was nothing but empty desks...no computers, no charts, no pens. Nothing.

"Ethan," she said slowly. "We're still in your dream, this isn't the Center."

Ethan was growing annoyed. "Of course it's the Center," he said. He grabbed Isla's arm and led her down the hallway to their father's office. He opened the door and ran around the desk toward their father. Michael scooped the boy up into his arms.

Maybe I'm the one who's confused, she thought.

"Isla love, you look tired," said Michael. "Ethan, I think we should put Isla to bed, don't you?"

Ethan nodded and suddenly the two of them were standing in Isla's bedroom.

Isla shrieked. She didn't like how everything kept changing. She sank down to the floor feeling defeated.

Ethan sat down next to her. "Isla, what is it?"

Isla sobbed as she placed her head between her knees. "I just want to go home."

"But…we are home," he said as he gestured around her room.

Isla buried her head deeper, losing all hope of convincing her brother he was dreaming.

Ethan had never seen his sister so vulnerable before and he wasn't sure what to do. He placed his arm on her shoulder.

Isla softened to his embrace as she leaned her head towards his, thinking about Mim with her brother Marcu.

"I'd love for us to be friends, Ethan."

"But you are my friend, Isla."

Isla examined her brother, his eyes seemed clearer. "Ethan, I feel like I'm going crazy. Is this a dream? Please tell me it's a dream."

Ethan's eyes welled with tears. "I don't like it here Isla, nothing's right. I don't know where we are either, but I just want everything to be back to normal. I'm glad that at least you're you again."

Isla wrapped her arms around her brother, relieved they were on the same team.

CHAPTER 24

Isla reached into her pocket for the handkerchief, hoping if she showed Ethan that she could change it into something else then maybe he'd believe her. Her face fell, remembering she had used it to hide them earlier. It must have been left in the forest when Ethan moved them. She noticed a deck of cards on her shelf. If there was one way to convince her brother, it would be with magic. She jumped up and grabbed the cards, pulling one off the top of the deck.

"I want you to focus really hard on a card and then tell me which card I'm holding."

Ethan did as instructed. "The ace of hearts."

Isla flipped the card around, hoping this worked. To her delight she was holding the ace of hearts.

Ethan sat up straighter. She had his full attention now. "Do it again."

Isla returned the card to the deck and shuffled the cards in front of her brother so he could see she wasn't cheating. When she finished she placed them in a pile in front of Ethan. He closed his eyes and thought about a different card. Isla flipped the top card. Ethan's eyes widened when he saw the one he'd been thinking about.

They did this a few more times as Ethan grew more and more astounded. "How are you doing this?"

"I'm not, Ethan. You are."

Of course she won't tell me, he thought, annoyed.

Isla put the deck in his hands. "Do the trick yourself," she suggested. "Take a card, decide what you want it to be, and then look at it."

Ethan did this a few times and each time pulled the exact card he had pictured. He peered at Isla suspiciously.

"It's not magic, Ethan. You can control the cards because we're in your dream."

He looked at her like she was crazy again.

"It's alright Ethan. I know…it doesn't make any sense."

She was acting too nice, like the other Isla that Ethan knew wasn't real and he wanted her to go away. Isla was staring at him quizzically. He squinted his eyes and thought harder about her being gone. Ethan wondered why he wasn't able to control her like he had earlier.

"What do you find most annoying about me?" Ethan asked.

Isla's eyes turned upward as she searched for the answer. "You really think I can name just one thing?"

Ethan giggled. He felt better. Nice Isla never would have said that, and he preferred real Isla anyway.

"Ethan, we need to get out of here before that creepy cloak cat finds us again. Or that man you saw."

Ethan grew agitated thinking about the man that had appeared out of nowhere. If this really was his dream, he certainly didn't dream that up. The man had long black hair that was tied back in a low ponytail and was wearing clothing that reminded Ethan of drawings he'd seen in history books of ancient tribes. He wore brown leather pants with a matching vest and had beaded cuffs with feathers sticking out of the top around each bicep. The man had picked up the magician's cloak and as they ran out of the house Ethan watched as it turned back into the odd cloak cat. When they made eye contact the man had looked just as startled as Ethan.

"We need to find Mim," said Isla, interrupting Ethan's thoughts.

"Mim?" he asked, perplexed.

"Yes, Mim. She's our grandmother...she's here too."

Ethan's face fell. Their grandmother never came to see them. This couldn't be Isla after all.

"Ethan, what's the matter?"

Ethan took a few steps away from the imposter, considering his options. Before he had time to come up with a plan he watched as the house behind Isla started to disappear piece by piece as if sucked into a tornado. Behind the missing pieces was nothing.

Isla turned to see what had caused the commotion and let out a loud scream. It seemed as though Ethan's dream realm was disappearing. "Run, Ethan! I don't want to know what happens if we get swallowed up by this."

Isla grabbed his arm and ran downstairs for the kitchen door. He was no longer concerned with how real she was, he just didn't want to get sucked up. Ethan threw open the door and raced out into the forest.

They ran and ran for what felt like an eternity, narrowly gaining ground on the black hole. When she felt like they had created enough distance from it, Isla turned towards her brother. Ethan stopped as she grabbed onto his arms and stared into his eyes. "Ethan, you're dreaming, you can stop this."

Ethan was gaping at something behind her again. She spun around and saw that the black hole was now coming from the other direction. "Oh no! Run!"

Ethan and Isla popped out of the forest into an open field. Isla was running furiously across the field when she saw figures in the distance coming out of the trees. She panicked and began to run in the other direction, but Ethan grabbed onto her arm and just shook his head.

"It doesn't matter which direction we go in," he said. "We might as well stop running."

Isla sank down with him. "I'm so sorry, Ethan. I've failed. I'm your big sister and I didn't protect you. I never should have made you fall from that tree and I shouldn't have yelled at you while you were on the swing. It's all my fault that we're even here."

There were tears in Ethan's eyes. This *was* his sister. He threw his arms around her neck. He was dreaming and somehow Isla was with him. "What do we do now?"

Isla's voice was frantic. "You have to make this stop, Ethan."

Ethan looked at the disappearing sky and wanted nothing more than for it to stop. He recalled the feeling he'd had when selecting the card he was thinking about from the deck. As the edges of the sky continued to fade from a pale blue to black, he focused on the outermost edge where it was black and willed it to turn to the pale blue color of the sky next to it.

Isla smiled when the sky stopped changing. "Ethan, you did it."

He continued to stare intently at the sky, knowing he hadn't accomplished what she was hoping. It was flickering from pale blue to black, like a light being switched on and off. He was fighting for control and knew the moment he stopped, the disappearing would continue. All he was doing was delaying the inevitable.

"Isla," Ethan started, his voice strained. "You need to get out of here while you still can. Go back to Dad."

"I'm not leaving you here, Ethan."

"Isla, it's okay."

"I'm not going anywhere," she said softly.

Ethan took his eyes off the sky for a second to look at his sister. A tear dripped down his cheek. "I don't know how long I can hold this, Isla. I can't let us both get swallowed up. Please, just go." He quickly looked back up at the sky and resumed fighting whatever was making his dream disappear.

Isla stood up and defiantly faced whoever had been coming out of the woods. Maybe she hadn't always done everything she could to help her brother in the past, but Isla wasn't going to let that stop her now. She couldn't believe it when she recognized Rae and Mim running across the field towards them. Isla was about to tell Ethan, but his ashen white face made her stomach drop. She glanced up at the sky, her breath caught in her throat when the disappearing continued.

"It's too strong, Isla."

Isla turned to the women and screamed as they disappeared into the nothingness. She dropped down to her brother and wrapped herself around his body, trying to shield him from whatever was coming. She squeezed her eyes shut tightly and held her breath.

"Ethan, open your eyes," he heard an unfamiliar voice say.

Ethan kept his eyes shut as he attempted to move his body. The weightless feeling he'd had before returned and he flailed around in a panic. His heart began thumping when he no longer felt Isla's arms around him. His eyes flew open.

In front of him was an old woman with dark, weathered skin. Her long white hair reached her waist and flowed around her body as if it were floating. She appeared to be translucent, like she wasn't completely there. Ethan looked around for Isla, but she wasn't with them. The old woman was the only thing he could see.

"Where is my sister? What have you done to Isla?"

The woman's voice was calm. "Your sister is fine. She is safe with your grandmother and Rae while you are here with me. They are not like you, child. They cannot come here."

"Why not? Where have you taken me?"

"I have brought you to what is known as Obscura."

"There's…there's nothing here."

"Indeed my boy, there's not. Although it's part of the dream realm, I cannot create dreams of my own here. In order for you to join me I had to pull you out of your dream. I'm afraid that's what was causing it to disappear."

Ethan felt terrified. His mind was racing, trying to figure out how to get away from the nothing and the strange woman.

"Please, do not be scared. I did not bring you here to harm you."

Ethan could sense the honesty in the woman's voice. She sounded almost desperate.

"My name is Amani and my people were known as the Iteiri. Long ago we were human, just like you, but terrible people killed us while we were in the dream realm, in Somnium. With no human bodies to return to, we all became trapped. Our consciousnesses slipped here...into Obscura."

"Where are your people now?" he asked, almost afraid to know the answer.

"For a time, my people made the best of our situation in Obscura. Many of us allowed our minds to go blank, entering a deep dreamless sleep. As time wore on though, a few wanted retribution for what had been done to us."

Amani paused and her face turned down. "They have learned how to control the dreams of the living, but because Iteiri are no longer part of the real world, they do so unseen. Some, like Nox, have learned to manipulate the dream he's in. Others are able to hold the dreamers in Somnium so they cannot wake. They are the reason you and your sister are trapped in your dream."

Ethan gasped. "If Iteiri can't be seen, how can I see you?"

"You, my child, you are different. You were born into both the real world and the dream realm the day your mother gave birth, which makes you a mystic. Until you fully accepted you were dreaming, until you accepted who you are, you weren't able to see us either. When you witnessed the cat returned to its original form, you finally began to realize that things weren't as they seemed. It's what caused you to see Nox in his human form. It is the reason he wants you."

CHAPTER 25

"That man…Nox…he's an Iteiri?" Ethan asked.

Amani nodded. "He created the cat because it was something you could see, something he could use to control you."

"But what could he possibly want from me?"

"It's not just you they want. They also need your sister. Nox and his followers have been searching for a way to enter the real world again. They want to go to Exsomnis. The only place they cannot enter is the space between the living and the dreaming, the darkness. They need Isla because she is a sleepwalker and she can leave Somnium without going through the darkness. They need you, because to a mystic, dreams are as real as the waking world."

"Why aren't you helping them? Don't you also want to return to Exsomnis?" he asked.

"We no longer belong in the real world. We have no human bodies to return to," Amani explained. "I have accepted this, but they have not. I refuse to fight them, but they must not be allowed to succeed."

"What am I supposed to do?"

"Nox kept you in Somnium waiting for this moment when you'd be able to see him. The only way out is to give him what he wants."

"But you just said I can't allow him to succeed," Ethan said, confused.

"You must not take him out of Somnium, but to be free you will need to break the hold they have over you."

"How?"

Amani's expression saddened. "There's nothing else I can do for you. I must return you to your dream now, to your sister."

Ethan's heart began pounding again, thinking about the moment that Isla had thrown herself on him as the nothing engulfed them. He didn't want to go back there. Ethan was about to ask more questions, but before he could open his mouth to speak, Amani said, "It's time."

Ethan wiggled a little under Isla's weight. She slowly unraveled from around her brother's body. She fearfully glanced up at the sky and was grateful it had returned to normal. A small smile spread across her face. Ethan followed his sister's gaze up towards the sky before it drifted down to the edges of the forest.

"We're not safe," he said.

Isla looked in the direction her brother was staring. "It's just Nurse Rae. And that's our grandmother, Mim." The women had reappeared and were now only about ten feet away.

"Not them." He pointed behind the two women at the edge of the field.

"Ethan, I don't see anyone else."

He covered his face with his hands. "I knew it. I knew you wouldn't believe me."

Isla gently took his hands and pulled them down. "I believe you Ethan. It's just that I don't see whatever you're pointing at."

Mim and Rae rushed to the children's sides. Mim gave Isla a quick hug. "I'm so sorry we didn't get to you sooner. When everything started disappearing, I was afraid to take us somewhere that was gone. We just started running and thankfully ended up here with you."

Mim addressed her grandson. "Ethan. I'm your grandmother, Mim. We're here to help you." He eyed her before turning back towards the edge of the field again.

"Ethan says there's something out there," Isla said. "Do you see anything?"

Mim and Rae both shook their heads no. "Tell us what you see Ethan," said Mim.

"It's the man I saw appear earlier. His name is Nox. Amani told me he's an Iteiri and that they want me and Isla to take them to the real world."

Isla raised an eyebrow and was about to question her brother, but when Rae and Mim both gasped she realized they knew what he was talking about.

Rae's eyes widened. "That can't actually be possible, can it? They'd just be dreams come to life. If it worked wouldn't they be…immortal."

"We cannot allow that to happen," said Mim.

The idea of a dream come to life terrified Ethan. He wished Nox were further away. He imagined a huge cavern in the ground between them and the Iteiri.

The field began opening up and crumbling before his eyes as a huge rift in the ground formed, Nox on one side and the four of them on the other.

"I'm afraid that won't stop him for long," said Rae.

Just as she predicted, they watched as one by one, huge rocks around the cavern began building up a bridge.

"What do we do now?" Isla asked.

Mim crouched down in front of Ethan. "Nox can only control what he can touch."

Ethan's gaze was brought back to the Iteiri when he saw that Nox had begun to cross the bridge. He quickly visualized a wall at the edge of the cavern. His face fell when not a moment later a hole was forming in the wall and Nox was coming through to the other side.

Ethan thought about being on a mountain peak so that they would be up high above where the Iteiri could reach. The ground below them began pushing upwards and soon they were on a hill the size of a tall building. Nox knelt down and touched the ground. Ethan groaned as the hill stopped growing and instead started shrinking towards the Iteiri.

Ethan was frantic. "It won't be long until we're right in front of him."

Rae knelt down and placed her own hands on the ground as she closed her eyes to focus. The shrinking slowed but they were still moving downwards.

"You're the only one who can make this stop," Isla said to her brother.

Ethan's mind was reeling with ideas, but if all that Nox needed was to touch his dream to change it he didn't know what else to do.

"I think I have an idea to buy us some time," said Rae. "Ethan, I'll need water. A lot of water."

Ethan surveyed the hill they were standing on and imagined they were at the top of a waterfall. The ground below their feet began receding, water pouring out. As the water approached Nox, he lifted his hands from the ground and in the direction of the falling water. As it passed through his hands the water spread and went around his body. He stood there for a moment before he dropped his hands and let the water flow over him again. He disappeared into the water and Ethan knew Nox must be breathing underwater just as he had done in the pool. The hill began shrinking down again.

Rae reached down and touched the top of the waterfall. She closed her eyes and imagined each drop of water turning into a mist and rising up like fog into the sky. If Nox wanted to make it go away, he'd have to touch each and every drop of water in his way.

"Can't you take us somewhere safe?" Isla asked Mim.

Mim focused before her expression became dismayed. "They still have a hold of both of you. I can't take you back to Exsomnis and there's not much else left to Ethan's dream." She turned to her grandson. "You have to make your dream bigger than this field."

Ethan peered into the fog, wondering how long it would take Nox to get to them. "We can't keep running. He's just going to keep chasing us. We need to get to the darkness. Amani said Iteiri can't go there."

"We can't get to the darkness either, not so long as they're holding us in Somnium," Isla protested, her eyes narrowing at her brother. He recognized the expression all too well—she thought he was being absurd. Ethan's confidence dropped, along with his shoulders. Isla immediately softened as she recognized what she had done. "What are you suggesting?" she asked, trying to sound encouraging.

Ethan quietly addressed the group. "He's not going to let us wake up until he gets what he wants, until we agree to bring him to Exsomnis. But the only way we can bring him there is if he lets us wake up."

Isla was beginning to understand what he was suggesting. "Ethan has a good point...Nox can't get what he wants without letting us go. There must be some way we can use that to our advantage."

Mim stared at Ethan and spoke almost through him. "Perhaps we can use the darkness?"

Ethan looked behind himself, but no one was there.

"Dr. Prasad can see Somnium through you," Rae explained.

"And Dad, well...Dad can keep us in the darkness," added Isla.

"The darkness...what is the darkness?" asked Ethan.

"The darkness is where we go when we aren't dreaming. It's a transition for our minds when we go from the real world to the dream realm," said Mim.

Ethan wondered if that's where he'd been when he felt like he was floating in nothing. "Can Dr. Prasad read my thoughts?"

"Not exactly. He sees what you see and feels what you're feeling, but he can't quite read your mind."

Ethan surveyed the group, it all finally made sense to him.

"Rae, you're like Nox. You touched the water and made mist. You can control what you touch?"

Rae nodded.

Ethan focused his attention on his grandmother. "You must have brought Rae here, so you're like Amani. You can bring people into dreams?"

Mim also nodded.

Ethan eyed his sister. "Amani said you're a sleepwalker, Isla. So you can be awake and asleep at the same time?"

"Yes," Isla said encouragingly.

"And that's why you can wake up without going through the darkness?"

"That's right," Isla said.

Ethan's face lit up. "I know what to do. You need to start sleepwalking."

CHAPTER 26

"Do you really think this'll work?" Michael asked Dr. Prasad, clearly distraught as he was told the plan.

Dr. Prasad shrugged his shoulders but kept his hand on Ethan. "It may be the best shot we have at getting them all safely out of there."

Isla gently placed a hand on her father's arm. "We can do this, Dad."

Michael placed his hand on top of hers as she said, "I have to walk him out. It's the only way Nox will let us go."

Isla squeezed her brother's hand as she got out of her bed and crouched down low behind it. She imagined it was a big boulder in Somnium that she could hide behind. Isla turned to the wall. Michael followed her gaze to the bears and balloons. He wished he could see what she was seeing.

"Ethan is going to let the fog down now, so we can find Nox," she explained.

Isla watched as Ethan stared into the fog that Rae had created. As he gazed into the mist it slowly started to clear. Ethan saw Nox sitting on the ground as though he had been waiting, the cloak cat at his side. The man looked up.

Ethan walked towards him with his hands up in the air, indicating they wanted a truce.

Mim and Rae stood still, staring at the small cloak cat in front of Ethan, trying to anticipate what might happen next. Before they knew what was happening, two ropes were climbing up their bodies at lightning speed. It encircled Rae's hands, pulling them away from her body before she had a chance to touch the rope and change it. Rae squirmed, fighting the tightening rope, but she couldn't move. She expected Mim to use her ability to get them out and became alarmed when she didn't. Mim shook her head. They were stuck.

Isla turned to her father from behind the rock and whispered, "Mim and Rae are trapped in some rope, I need a way to get them out."

Michael instinctively reached into his pants for his pocketknife and then remembered he had already given it to Isla. He frantically searched the room when his eyes landed on some scissors. They were small, but extremely sharp. He grabbed the scissors and handed them to Isla.

Isla spotted some wires on Ethan's bedside table and wrapped one around the scissors. She brought her attention to the field, imagining the wire was a small snake. She sent the snake and the scissors through the grass, watching as it slithered up Rae's body and down her arm. Rae squeezed her eyes shut tight and held her breath, terrified.

The snake stopped in Rae's hand, pressing the cold metal into her palm. Rae peeked through her eyelashes at the snake and saw the scissors. Isla let the snake drop to the ground. Rae exhaled deeply before she rotated the scissors back towards her arm, furiously cutting at the vine around her wrist.

"Isla, look out!" Dr. Prasad yelled as he caught movement out of the corner of Ethan's eye.

It was too late. Isla watched in horror as the cloak cat grew to the size of a huge jaguar. The jaguar quickly pounced on her, knocking her to the ground. She gasped as the weight of the enormous cat pressed into her chest. Isla froze, terrified as the golden coins seemed to stare into her eyes.

Michael reached out for his daughter as she stiffened, struggling to breathe. He looked at Dr. Prasad in desperation. "Amit?"

"She's been found."

Michael slouched down on the floor, cradling his daughter. "I've got you, Isla. I'm right here with you."

Isla was still grasping onto her brother's hand in the hospital bed, but Michael felt her take his hand with the other and squeeze it firmly.

The jaguar grabbed Isla's shirt and dragged her across the ground towards Ethan and Nox. Isla tried scrambling to her feet, but it was no use. She screeched in pain as her skin scraped against rocks and branches.

At the sound of his daughter's screams Michael protectively wrapped himself around her body as tears ran down his face. His eyes went black as he once again tried to pull them to the darkness, but it was no use.

The jaguar dropped Isla abruptly and then shrunk down to the size of a house cat. It purred, weaving back and forth between Ethan's legs. Ethan stumbled away from the creature and ran to Isla's side to help her stand up. He imagined them being behind Nox, and in the blink of an eye they had moved.

Nox grinned. "This isn't going to end how you think it will, child. It's best you give up now."

Rae and Mim, now free, approached the black cat. Ethan saw their confusion as they tried to determine exactly where Nox was. He glowered at the Iteiri and imagined he was inside a cage. The moment his location was visible, the women ran to attack. Rae reached for Mim and together they placed their hands on the cage.

Mim closed her eyes and imagined the small piece of land Ethan had created for this moment. They opened their eyes and looked around at the vast nothingness around them. They quickly let go of the cage as Mim closed her eyes, thinking of the field they had just left.

They opened their eyes to find themselves still in the forest. The field was gone.

"Where are they?"

Mim felt frustrated she hadn't seen this coming. "It's like before…everything has changed. I'm afraid the children are on their own."

CHAPTER 27

Ethan and Isla huddled together, terrified. They were back in the forest surrounded by dense trees. Everything was dark except for the faint moonlight shining through the branches, casting an eerie glow on the ground. There were sounds coming from all around, crickets chirping, wings flapping as bats flew by. It felt like everything was closing in on them. Ethan jumped as Isla accidentally stepped on a branch and it cracked.

Isla tried to understand how this had all happened. In the blink of an eye, Nox had removed himself from the cage as if he had known what was coming. The moment Mim and Rae were gone Nox had dropped to the ground to touch the earth below him. Trees shot up from the ground all around them.

"Ethan, do something," Isla whispered.

Her brother stood motionless. "I...I can't," he said, squeezing his eyes shut.

Nox knew exactly what he was doing. Isla felt helpless. She stood in front of her brother protectively.

"Please," she cried out, not knowing where the Iteiri was. "I'll do whatever you want, just stop this."

Everything around them went silent. Nox was listening.

"I'll walk him out. That's what you want isn't it?"

Ethan put his hand on Isla's arm.

Isla was in tears. "I'm so sorry Ethan, this is all my fault." She heaved in a few breaths through her fear. "I'm not going to let him keep doing this to you!"

Ethan stared at his sister intently. "It's time we go home to Dad, Isla. We have to do what Nox wants. It's the only way."

Something about the way he was looking at her made her pause. It felt like he was trying to coax her into reading his mind. *It's time we go home to Dad.*

Isla focused on the Center. *How can Dad help us?* It didn't make sense.

Isla glanced up at Dr. Prasad who gave her a slow, encouraging, nod. She felt her father's hand give her a soft squeeze and suddenly she understood what Ethan was suggesting. She brought her attention fully back to Somnium. Ethan placed his hand in hers.

Nox took Ethan's other hand. "It's time," he said.

"Now, Isla," Ethan said.

Isla again focused on the Center and glanced over at her brother lying still in the hospital bed before she squeezed her father's hand a little tighter. She watched as Somnium began to fade. Nox really had let them go. She continued pulling them out of Somnium but stopped abruptly when she saw the form of a man materializing in the room next to Ethan's bed.

The man appeared stunned as they made eye contact. He looked down at his body, in awe that it had really worked. Nox pulled a feather from one of the bands around his arms and gently blew it out of his hand. He watched as it drifted through the air and landed on Ethan's bed. Nox eyed the boy lying in the bed, still sound asleep. He glowered at Isla suspiciously.

"Dad, now!" Isla cried out.

In an instant, everything disappeared.

Isla inhaled sharply as her entire body tensed. Her eyes flew open and she sat up straight in bed, trying to figure out where she was.

"It's okay, you just woke up," she heard her father say.

Isla looked around the familiar room at the Center, noting the teddy bears and balloons. She saw Mim sitting in a chair, smiling at her. Isla's gaze fell on her brother's bed. It was empty.

Isla jumped up. "Where's Ethan?"

"He's fine Isla," her father said. "He's awake. Nurse Rae just took him out for a walk."

"You mean…it worked?"

"It did, but not exactly as we planned. Thankfully when the Iteiri let you go I was able to pull you all to the darkness—it must have sent Nox back to wherever he came from. You've been asleep for—" He consulted his watch. "Eighteen hours now. It would seem your body needed time to recover."

Mim got up from her chair and put an arm around her granddaughter. "You must be starving, dear."

"I could use some breakfast," Isla admitted.

"Why don't you two head to the cafeteria and I'll have Nurse Rae bring Ethan over," Michael suggested.

Isla glanced down at her pajamas but was too hungry to care what anyone thought. She grabbed a sweatshirt and joined Mim.

When they arrived at the cafeteria, Isla immediately grabbed a chocolate chip muffin and put in on her tray. A moment later she grabbed a second one.

Just as Isla and Mim were about to sit down, Isla saw Rae coming through the entryway, pushing Ethan in a wheelchair. Michael and Dr. Prasad weren't far behind. Isla squealed as she ran over to her brother and gave him a hug. Ethan wrapped his arms around her, glowing from the unexpected attention.

Isla hugged Rae too. She then took the handles of the wheelchair and gave her brother a tip back as she raced off to the table. Ethan giggled as he held on for dear life.

Isla sat down next to him and handed him one of her chocolate chip muffins. "I knew you'd want one too."

Ethan's eyes welled with tears.

"Don't go getting all mushy on me, it's just a muffin."

Ethan felt a little overwhelmed. He lifted the feather he'd been carrying around all morning and twirled it in his fingers, looking at Isla. "Did you leave this on my bed?" he asked. "No one seems to know where it came from."

Isla nearly choked on the piece of muffin in her mouth. "That," she tried to say through her coughing. "That came from Nox. It's from Somnium."

CHAPTER 28

A month later, Isla was helping pack up her brother's belongings at the Center when Mim walked into the room. Isla glanced up from the box she was filling with stuffed animals and smiled.

"Are we all ready, then?" Mim asked.

"So ready!" Isla said excitedly. "I can't wait to bring Ethan home...it's been far too long." Isla walked over to the window and picked up the last remaining stuffed animal and tossed it into a box. She surveyed the room and felt grateful knowing it was the last time she'd be seeing it for a while.

Isla picked up the box and headed out into the hallway with Mim. As they pushed through the entrance Isla saw her father at the curb with the car. He opened up the trunk but it was packed to the brim with Ethan's stuff. Isla couldn't help but giggle at the huge squished up teddy bear face that was smiling up at her.

"It's okay Dad, I can sit with it in my lap." Isla slid into the back seat with the box and struggled to maneuver her seat belt across her body in the limited space.

"Let me help," Ethan offered. Isla warmed at the gesture from her brother and handed him the buckle. He pulled it through and pushed it into the latch.

"Ta-da!" he said.

Isla smirked at her brother. She was often surprised by how her relationship with Ethan had changed. She knew that before the accident if Ethan had offered to help her she would have been quick to dismiss him. After their experience together in Somnium though, she realized he wasn't the useless little kid she had often thought he was.

"Thanks Ethan," she said sincerely.

Her brother seemed lost in thought as he stared at the forest behind the Center. Isla reached over and grabbed his hand. She desperately wanted him know that everything was going to be fine. Ethan's gaze fell to his lap and Isla worried that maybe he didn't believe it.

Mim spun around from the front seat. "You must be excited to return to your friends at school," she said to her grandson. Ethan perked up and began talking about all his friends and how great it was that they had all been visiting the last few weeks. Almost every day, someone new had dropped by to play with Ethan. It had helped to improve his spirits and encourage him to get better.

Ethan's body had grown weak from being in a coma, so he had to attend physical therapy every day to regain his strength. The rest of his time was spent with a tutor to help him catch up on schoolwork.

For the first week after the coma, Ethan had been terrified of going back to sleep, scared that the Iteiri would return. It took some time, but they were finally able to convince him that there was nothing to be afraid of in the darkness. So long as Michael was catching their dreams, the Iteiri were powerless. Ethan eventually became more comfortable with sleeping, but he was still haunted by the idea of Nox returning.

Ethan beamed as they pulled into the driveway of their home. Everyone quickly jumped out of the car, excited to accompany him into the house. Michael unlocked the front door and ushered his son inside. Ethan's memories of the specific dreams he'd had in Somnium had long since faded, but the forest in his father's office was difficult to forget. His apprehension disappeared when he walked into the foyer and saw his father's mahogany desk. Ethan ran up to his room and sat on his bed. He didn't realize how wonderful being home would feel.

Later, the four ate dinner together and made small talk about returning to their normal lives. Isla attempted to make a joke that "nothing would be *normal* again," but instead of the chuckles she expected, everyone became quiet.

Isla broke the silence. "No one seems to want to talk about it, but we all know that the Iteiri are still out there. I mean, what even happened to Nox?"

"I'm guessing he was returned to Obscura, but unfortunately we don't really know," said Mim.

"That feather seems to mean we can do what they want. We did what Mom said we would—we brought dreams to life," said Isla.

Michael quietly contemplated that Shayla had also seen them bring Iteiri to life. He wondered if that would also come to pass.

"I know that you're worried about Ethan and I being in Somnium, Dad," Isla continued, "But we both want to learn more from Mim...we need to."

Taken aback, Michael looked up from his plate. He focused on Ethan. "Are you sure about this?" he asked.

"No," Ethan admitted. "But the Iteiri aren't just going to go away. They'll find a way to get to us again. I can't let them hurt anyone else when it's me they're after."

Michael's face was sad thinking about what they had been through. "I don't like it, but you're right. The best way to protect you both is for you to understand what you can do in Somnium, and Mim is the best person to help you with that. Now that we know dreams really can be brought to Exsomnis, Mim and I think perhaps there's a way I can bring the darkness to Somnium. If the Iteiri can't enter where the darkness is, then it would make Somnium safe for you. As soon as we figure that out, you can go back."

Mim was thoughtful for a few moments. She beamed at her grandchildren. "Until then, you need to spend some time being exactly what you aren't…normal."

ACKNOWLEDGEMENTS

Joel - you tirelessly read every single version of this book…to say you've been an instrumental piece in finishing it is a huge understatement. You turned my vision of the cape kitty into a work of art, I couldn't be more pleased with the cover.

Ariana & Lukas - I wrote this book in the hopes of teaching you both a lesson. In the end I've learned so much from both of you. Ariana - your enthusiasm has been infectious. You encouraged me to keep going even when it seemed like I was never going to finish. Lukas - you provided me with so many thoughtful ideas for this book. Your natural talent for storytelling helped me improve my own writing.

Dad - I can't tell you how much having a tangible book to hold meant to me. It changed everything.
Mom - your feedback after reading this book made me believe I had done something worthy of printing.
Greg, Fabiana & Breanna - your feedback each step of the way helped make my dream a reality.

ABOUT THE AUTHOR

For much of her adult life Angelia has been a sleepwalker. Although she has never done anything dangerous, like leave the house or drive a car, she has been known to get up in the middle of the night and change her clothing. She frequently wakes her husband with tales of mysterious things occurring, like lasers shooting around the room, spiders climbing up the walls, and even murals that move. Her experiences provided a lot of inspiration for the Somnium series.

Angelia's parents have always encouraged her to step out of her comfort zone, particularly when it comes to doing things herself. Among the many DIY projects she's completed are replacing plumbing, demoing a bathroom, and making furniture.

Angelia enjoys following in her grandmother's footsteps by planting a vegetable garden each summer. She may not have the green thumb that her grandmother had, but with her daughter's help she was able to recreate Thelma's to-die-for sweet pickles using her own homegrown cucumbers.

Made in the USA
Coppell, TX
06 April 2021

53222177R00128